Thank you for picking up this book, please enjoy it, or at least try to... You want to hear about Alicia? So meet her. Alicia has completed one year of English at university, and she is fully planning on finishing her degree. Alicia kind of fell from three-storey building, so she is in a clinic getting better, slowly but surely. Currently she can't walk, talk, eat or drink and she can't move her left arm. So that has given her plenty of time for writing, hence how this book has come about...

Alicia King

LET IT SNOW

AUSTIN MACAULEY PUBLISHERS
LONDON • CAMBRIDGE • NEW YORK • SHARJAH

Copyright © Alicia King 2023

The right of Alicia King to be identified as author of this work has been asserted by the author in accordance with sections 77 and 78 of the Copyright, Designs and Patents Act 1988.

All rights reserved. No part of this publication may be reproduced, stored in a retrieval system, or transmitted in any form or by any means, electronic, mechanical, photocopying, recording, or otherwise, without the prior permission of the publishers.

Any person who commits any unauthorised act in relation to this publication may be liable to criminal prosecution and civil claims for damages.

This is a work of fiction. Names, characters, businesses, places, events, locales, and incidents are either the products of the author's imagination or used in a fictitious manner. Any resemblance to actual persons, living or dead, or actual events is purely coincidental.

A CIP catalogue record for this title is available from the British Library.

ISBN 9781528969413 (Paperback)
ISBN 9781528969444 (ePub e-book)

www.austinmacauley.com

First Published 2023
Austin Macauley Publishers Ltd®
1 Canada Square
Canary Wharf
London
E14 5AA

Chapter 1

She exhaled, deeply, she knew what she was going to do, she had a plan, an evil little plan, this wasn't her first rodeo, if only weed didn't mess with her head now because if it didn't, she would've already smoked a joint, which would've helped with the pain. Not that she really wanted it to, but it would have helped with the pain, it was an advantage of getting high, I guess. Get high to escape those low feelings? Well, in this instance, she would be escaping the low feeling of pain. But no, not now… She wanted to feel pain, well to feel something… Anything… She even accepted pain…

A single, solitary tear escaped her eye, how poetic! She was now ready, well, she was as ready as she would ever be…Maybe ready is the wrong word…She was there, the knife was there, yeah, there is a better word, not ready…

The knife was already in her hand, she knew her task, she was there, she was prepared, well, she was as prepared as she was ever going be, so she pressed the knife's blade against her wrist and sliced along it, it was already quite cut up, it didn't feel good, no good is the wrong word…But it felt like a release. Physical pain to counteract mental pain?

Yes, that's one way to describe it, another way to describe it is messing up your wrist so you have to cover it up all the time, so no one can see it, so no one asks any questions…Yes, that's better…She was good at covering it up, well, she had been having to do it for years…She did a few more cuts because why do one when you can do multiple? But each one felt like a release, bizarrely.

The blood could've been a metaphor for pain and it was flowing out of her. Ha, self-harm doesn't really feel like the way to start a story, but here we are…

That was her bedtime routine finished, most people might read, but oh no, not Kat. Cutting was far more interesting than any book. So, like usual, she put the knife hidden away, it was out of sight, but most definitely not out of mind, she got in bed, lay down on her side and went to sleep, whilst clutching her messed up wrist with her more normal, other hand.

No one knew she self-harmed and she planned to keep it that way, well, apart from her boyfriend, it's a little hard to hide when you're naked in front of someone, but it's not like she wanted to tell him. He didn't even try to stop her from doing it so that just mentally reinforced the, quite frankly, wrong belief that cutting yourself was OK.

Oh, life is just so hard for a teenager, IT'S JUST SO HARD, well, actually in Kat's case it was, (do you like how I called her Kat? For the sole purpose that it sounds like cut for self-harm, this story is actually about Barack Obama, oh no wait, no it isn't, you'll never get her real name out of me, NEVER) she was still a little baby, what with only being fifteen and all and she already had two suicide attempts under her belt, with whatever drugs she had stored away. One was copious amounts of MDMA, boy did she feel it and feel the high effects after and the other was copious amounts of cocaine, she was hoping to overdose, not just get really high.

Well, she didn't get high at all with the cocaine because she decided to ingest it. They didn't work, obviously, I mean she's still alive. She didn't exactly fall asleep early on either of those nights, but waking up was always awful, to say she cried was putting it lightly. There seems to be a negative theme occurring here with bedtime, which is strange because she loves sleeping, so much so that she would happily do it forever...

In the same house, downstairs, her parents were snorting fat lines of cocaine, no that comes later, but don't you worry, it comes...They were only watching TV. I wonder if they knew just how depressed their daughter was. She kept the depression a deliberate secret, I'm sorry she was past the point of just being sad, miserable was a better adjective, no fuck it, depressed is better...

I wonder, would they have taken the old habit back up and involved their daughter if they knew? It's not even about them taking the old habit back up, they're adults, they can do what they want, but involving their child? No, I think that's where the line crosses from OK to fucked...

This weekend, on the Saturday, so in two days' time, was her dad's fortieth birthday party so they would have many people over at the house to celebrate, including her boyfriend, who was the son of a family friend, who used to work with her dad. She was looking forward to seeing him, they even had each other's virginities. Aw, how sweet! Young love! Um, how about no, you won't be saying that by the end of this story, trust me...Oh boy, does he fuck up...Saying it was a mistake, was too small...

But for now, she loved him, so was looking forward to seeing him because he hadn't fucked up yet...He would come over for the whole weekend, starting early Saturday. He lived a few hours' drive away, so she couldn't see him every day, so it was always exciting when she got to see him.

She dreamed strange dreams that night, they were quite a common occurrence for her, I guess you could call it a side effect of self-harm…Ha or maybe she was just strange…? Or maybe it was both things mixed together…

OK, maybe her dreams weren't so much strange as depressing, really quite depressing, she may have died in her dream, oh no, wait, that's what she wanted, so surely that would've been a good dream? Or was she put in pain? No, again that was what she wanted. What would make her sad? I know! If she lost her iPod, music was a big part of her life. So, she had an awful dream because she lost her iPod. Go on, guess if her dream put her in a good mindset for the next day? Go on, guess. I'm listening…

She begrudgingly awoke because of her alarm the next day. She woke up and jumped out of bed! She was ready to take on and face the day! Oh no, wait, no, she wasn't. She realised it was school, so she put her head down and screamed into a pillow instead. She was nothing if not productive…

Oh, how she wished she lost her iPod now in real-life, she could get music elsewhere, if it meant she could miss school she thought whilst thinking of her dream. It was basically her baby, so of course, her parents would let her miss school…Maybe…Possibly…Well, she could try praying that they would let her miss school…But it was quite unlikely…

She put on her school uniform, slowly, so as not to hurt her wrist, but wasn't pain the whole point of messing it up in the first place? Oh no, time and place? But wasn't the place in her bedroom? As in where she was right now? Oh no, wait, the time was wrong, it wasn't bedtime. But for school didn't she do up her face up all good and proper with make-up, like everyone else?

Oh, wait no she didn't, no make-up, first, sleep was more important than having time to put on make-up and two, she was going to a party later so would put on make-up then. Why would she be bothered about how she looked at school? Her boyfriend didn't even go there? So, normal unmade-up face it was because she wasn't even remotely bothered. Her face was a mess, her wrist was a mess, she was a mess. Yep, check, check and check, she was all ready for school. A magical holy trinity…

When she was just about ready, well, there were now clothes on her body, so she was presentable, she went downstairs, it was time to break the fast, sorry is that too complicated for you to understand? It was her breakfast time. She made herself a bowl of cereal and sat down at the Kitchen table and played some awful game on her phone while she sat and ate.

She checked the time, it was twenty past seven, time to vacate the premises, her coach came at half past. So it was time to leave, she practically inhaled the last few mouthfuls of her cereal, stood up, put her bowl in the dishwasher, went upstairs, grabbed her school bag, left the house and made her merry way to her coach stop. Blimey, that felt like a big, long sentence, so many commas.

Next time maybe don't explain everything she does, I think it's quite obvious, it's not like she was going to just magically fly and appear at school, is it? OK, forget all that…Forget that sentence…She then plugged herself into her iPod by putting her headphones on, thank God, it wasn't lost, she needed it and she smoked a post-breakfast cigarette on her way to the coach stop, so what if she wasn't yet eighteen? She wasn't hurting anything, well, apart from her young lungs…

When she arrived at the coach stop, she waited patiently for her coach to stop and show up. Hey, wait a minute. What was wrong with the roads? It took forever to show up; oh no, wait; no, it didn't, that must've been a different coach. Oops. My bad. It only went and bloody came on time. As per.

Annoyingly, it was not even remotely late, it was like clockwork. The journey took around three-quarters of an hour, so plenty of time to socialise with other people on the coach! Shame she wasn't remotely bothered by socialising, she just remained plugged into her iPod, socialising was just too much to ask from her this early in the morning, aw bless! She was still half asleep. So, she kept her eyes just staring out the window…

Fuck knows why but she was feeling instrumental music this morning, I guess hearing people talk, even on tape, was too much for her. The journey didn't feel particularly slow or quick, just normal, but they got there, unfortunately, to the emporium of learning! Well, school…Still listening to music she trudged off the coach, but before she did so, she breathed in and breathed out deeply, who knows why she felt she had to steady herself, it was just school, going had been a regular occurrence for years, you know, since she was about four. But steady her breathing, she did.

She kept the trudging up as she walked into school because why walk normally?

'Are you ready for Ryan's party thing, that's too small to be a party tonight?' Her best friend asked her. What are the odds? Walking into school at the same time?

'If by that, what you really mean to ask me is have you acquired some not-so-legal substances, to make tonight's shindig better, then yes, yes I have.'

'Perfect.'

'You know it wouldn't kill you to pick up once in a while, you take enough?' Kat said quite strongly and snorted and took a line of air for dramatic effect.

'That may be, but I'm pretty sure picking up is illegal so I'm not sure I feel comfortable doing it, whereas putting something in your own body is just putting something in your own body?'

'Not sure if that's quite how it works but OK, whatever floats your boat...Good to know you think it's fine for me to break the law...?' Kat laughed as she replied.

'Living that thug life,' her best friend said and laughed.

They then walked into school together, yes, Kat was walking normally now, not trudging, maybe it's because she liked her best friend or something...Who knows...

'See you at break time,' the best friend said and walked into her form room to get registered, let's call her Juliet because her parents love Shakespeare, so Romeo and Juliet, bit of a weak protagonist to name your daughter off but OK. Well, I suppose even though they love King Kong they couldn't exactly name their daughter King Kong...Would've raised many a question...

Kat continued the normal walk up to her own form room on her lonesome, well, she didn't fly because she couldn't and the trudging didn't return. Result! When she got there, she sat in her usual seat at the back because she was never ready to really socialise and took only one headphone out of her ear, just in case anyone spoke to her. She desperately hoped they wouldn't, but just in case. Her eyes were now finally clear of sleep.

She was happy that her eyes now felt clear, but miserable in other ways, having sleep in her eyes was the least of her problems in the grand scheme of things…I mean come on? School she could cope with, but other things in her life? Not so much…It was just a normal day in her form, not much chit-chat was occurring.

Upon seeing not much talking was taking place, Kat put her second headphone back in her ear, but annoyingly, within seconds, Ryan who was in her form and who was having the party tonight, OK, it was not big enough to be called a party, it was more of a gathering. But he almost waited just until both her headphones were in her ears to talk to her.

He was sweet, he fancied her secretly, hence why she got an invite, they weren't exactly close, but even if she didn't have a boyfriend, he had no chance of getting with her 'are you looking forward to tonight? You are coming right?' Ryan asked; aw, how sweet! If that doesn't mean he wanted her there, I don't know what does…Maybe, he liked her or something? Who knows…Well, we do know but that's beside the point…

She didn't want to, but she took out the same single headphone from her ear that she took out earlier so she could hear. She practically glared at Ryan as she did so.

'Repeat. Headphones. Couldn't hear.'

'Oh God, I'm sorry, no forget it, feel free to plug yourself back in.'

'I've already freed my ear, so go for it, but if you were wondering, yes I will be dropping a pill tonight.'

'Does that mean you're coming?'

'You know what I don't know, I heard on the street was a great place to pop pills; yes, of course, I'm coming you ding nut.'

'Sweet. Cool beans. Just thought I'd check...'

'Does that mean I can plug myself back in?' Without even knowing it she was going for the treat them mean, keep them keen approach.

'Yes, of course, you can, I apologise for interrupting...' He walked away and went back to his seat, so she plugged her other headphone back into her ear and maybe got to listen to about ten seconds of the song that was playing with full immersion, uninterrupted. But then the school bell rang, to signify the start of the school day.

Oh, this pissed Kat off, school was such an annoyance, it was so unfair, why couldn't she just listen to music, uninterrupted, all day? In anger, she threw her iPod and headphones at the wall in front of her. She just wanted peace and quiet, why was that so hard?

Surprise, surprise, Ryan was the one to pick it up. How sweet! No, not really...How typical was better...

'Hey did you drop this?' he said, picked it up and put it on the desk in front of her.

'Ugh, yes, it's so irritating whenever I drop something it always seems to launch itself with force in front of me.'

'Ha.'

Was his reply but he didn't laugh, he just left the room and went to his lesson, so she did the very same. What did she have first? She checked her timetable, double Chemistry, oh joy! She liked her class but didn't like the teacher, fuck knows how she was going to pass a GCSE in Chemistry? Was she ever going to use a Bunsen Burner outside of Chemistry class?

I think not...What did GCSE even stand for? Gifted Cabbages Secrete Excellence? Those cabbages sound impressive, I mean wow.

The walk to Chemistry was bog standard and boring, why couldn't this school day be over? But it hadn't even really begun yet...Chemistry, just like the walk, was bog standard and boring, hey there's a theme occurring here with school...They didn't even do an experiment, they just took notes, for the full double period.

Well, Kat didn't just take notes, she coloured all of her Chemistry book with a beautiful shade of black. When the lesson eventually finished it was break, time to see her best friend, they weren't in the sixth form yet, so they weren't yet allowed to leave school for a cigarette, but luckily they had discovered you could sneakily smoke on the roof of the Science Block, unnoticed. Approximately ten seconds into the start of break, Kat received a text from her best friend, Juliet.

Where you at, ma nigga?

How poetic...

I'll be where we usually smoke.

Was Kat's reply.

So she left her classroom, but let everyone else leave to go downstairs and go to the Dining Hall, to get some food and go to break first, to once again break the fast, once the coast was clear she went up the last flight of stairs to the roof. She sat down and typically rolled herself a cigarette, just when it was rolled her best friend swung open the door, decided to let her presence be known and made an appearance.

'Maths is not for me, swear down.' Was the first thing Juliet said, as she came over to Kat and sat herself down.

'I know right, they invented calculators for a reason.'

'Preach it, Sister.'

The two girls lit their cigarettes, Juliet smoked straights so didn't have to spend time worrying about rolling.

'So what do you want to do drug-wise tonight?' Was the first thing Kat said, you know she was good at asking the real questions…

'OK, so is that goodbye to talking about the lessons we just had? You know normal chit-chat? Let's just dive into talking about drugs…'

'Sorry, you've already expressed your disdain with maths, what more is there to say?'

'Conversations generally work two ways, here's an idea you could talk about you.' Juliet almost laughed as she said it.

'OK, if I must, ready? I'll give you two words Chemistry and boring.'

'How poetic.'

'Why thank you, so let me ask my slightly more serious question again, ready? OK. So what do you want to do drug-wise tonight?'

'I don't know? The usual?'

'See, that wasn't so hard to answer, was it?'

Juliet didn't even grace that with a verbal response, she saw violence as the answer, so she punched Kat in the shoulder instead.

'Ow, unnecessary!'

'Oh sorry, I thought I saw a fly on you. My bad.'

Kat also didn't even grace that with a verbal response, but she didn't resort to violence either, she saw glaring as a much more effective response also, she was so similar to her best friend, aw how sweet. But she didn't resort to violence, she just glared at her violent friend instead. Probably better that way…

Chapter 2

Then, suddenly, a younger boy practically ran onto the roof, there were tears in his eyes, he ran to the edge of the roof and stood on the edge overlooking the ground. He hadn't even noticed the two smoking girls. It really looked like he wanted to jump, so Juliet stood up, got rid of her cigarette and backed away, slowly.

'I'm just going to get a teacher,' she whispered and stopped slowly backing away and just sprinted away instead.

'Hey, come back! Don't just leave me here by myself,' Kat said to nothing because Juliet had already sprinted away. But the boy heard her, he turned around, he was obviously hoping to be alone.

'Don't come near or I'll do it, I'll jump.'

She saw herself as now, unfortunately, involved, so she got up and walked towards him with disdain, but not too close, so as not to freak him out. How was she going to talk to him? If the roles were reversed, what would've helped her?

'Just so you know you've now involved me, thanks for that, so the least you can do is talk to me before jumping...'

'Back away! Don't try to stop me!'

He turned back to stare at the ground.

'No, I'm not going to try and stop you. How would I anyway?' Kat put her hands up to signify innocence, but he didn't even look back. 'It's your life or your death, you can do what you want.' She took a step closer to him. 'I just want a conversation with you before you do anything, please? With cherries on top?'

He wiped his eyes, because he hadn't just magically stopped crying and nodded slowly. Progress!

Kat then spoke again, 'My first question is fairly obvious, would you like to guess what it is?'

He shook his head; he just couldn't speak at this moment in time.

'OK, so tell me, why are you here?'

'We're kids, we have to go to school.'

Kat actually laughed at that. 'I'll be sure to make a note of that, suicidal boy has a sense of humour…'

He joined in with the laughter and laughed at that also. 'Ugh, OK fine, life is just too hard. I just can't, I'm done…'

'I know it is, trust me I know it is. Look at me.'

He turned around to look at her and she lifted her sleeve and showed him her wrist, no not the normal one…

'Fuck, are you OK?'

'Been better. I've also got a few attempts in me, so don't think you're alone…I'm fully aware of how hard life can be.'

'I'm past the point of caring if I'm alone.'

'That may be, you may not care, but I don't even know you properly and it's safe to say you're not alone with me and you can always talk to me, you might even find an outside perspective to be useful…'

His tears were flowing even more strongly now, but he still was able to get a question out, 'How have you tried?'

'Trying to overdose on various drugs.'

'Fuck, why didn't it work?'

She laughed and just about got some words out, 'You know what, I don't know why it didn't work, let me just go and ask my crystal ball.'

'You're not funny.'

'Oh, but I am; if you can be suicidal, I can be funny.'

They both laughed at that.

Her cigarette had finished ages ago but she still held onto it, she needed to hold on to something… To ground her.

'I think I needed to meet you here like this, it's not exactly a happy meeting but it was necessary…' he said.

'Whoa, whoa, wait, have I succeeded? Does that mean you're going to step away from the edge of the building now?'

'I think so, yeah…'

'Thank God, I hope you know you've not only saved your own life, but you've also saved mine too, oh lord if you had jumped, I would not have been able to cope, I would have most likely jumped too…'

He laughed. 'This isn't about you, no offence.'

'Yes, it is. Everything is about me?'

'I take back what I said about needing to meet you…'

'WHY? BUT EVERYTHING IS ABOUT ME?'

'How have I just let you talk me out of jumping?'

As if to really prove his point, he gingerly stepped away from the edge of the roof and into Kat's arms.

'Ha, smoking may kill but it just saved a life because it brought me here, they've got the advertising all wrong.'

'Can I have one?'

'One what?'

'A cigarette?'

She pushed him away from her. 'Whoa, whoa, wait, I just saved your life and you're asking me for something that will kill you in a slower, much more painful way?'

'That's certainly one way of putting it.'

'OK, just so long as you know.'

She had her mission, roll. One for her and one for her new friend, she passed him the freshly rolled cigarette.

'Cheers,' he said, he held it strangely, I don't think he had ever smoked before. Aw, he was just a kid.

She quickly rolled her smoke, in a matter of seconds, I think she had done this before…She went to sit down where she had sat before, before being so rudely interrupted and he did the same. She lit hers and passed him the lighter, he didn't set himself on fire! He was able to light it! Get in my son! It was all going so well for him, well, that was until he inhaled a drag…Boy, did it make him cough. Quite a lot.

She laughed. 'Jeez, no you got it all wrong, they cause a slow death.'

He was still coughing but he was now laughing as well. He stubbed the cigarette out; he had given up trying to smoke it.

'I don't think smoking is for me.'

'It's OK, I know the truth, you can say it, you just really want to live life now? No jumping and no cancer?'

'You're lucky I like you.'

'Lucky you like me? Really? No, I believe the definition of lucky is winning the lottery or something, where's my money? No offence you're OK, I guess, but you're not that good…' They both laughed at that.

'But my mother always tells me I'm like a million bucks?'

'No, no, no,' Kat tutted whilst trying to keep a straight face, 'she's lying to herself and more importantly, she's lying to you…'

'You can't just make decisions about my mother; you haven't even met her.'

Her response was a smile. Then she said, 'Look at me smoking in school, I do what I want. If I want to make decisions about your mother, I can and will.'

'OK, good point, well made.'

'Why thank you. I think we're at the point for introductions, aren't we? I saved your life, so I saved your name so please give me your name at least?'

He laughed. 'My name? Bob The Builder.'

'No, be serious.'

'Of course, you don't know who I am, my bad, but when I'm not at the top of a building, I go by the name Dominic, I'm in the year below you, so I assume that's probably why you don't know me, but I know who you are, it's Kat right?'

Kat laughed. 'To assume makes an ass out of you and me…'

'Kat, you should really grow up…'

'Wait, how do you know who I am?' She now felt cautious.

'Like I said year below, don't you know some people's names in the year above you without actually knowing them?'

'OK fair. I was worried there, for a second there I thought you were not only suicidal but a stalker freak as well.'

'Just saying, I appreciate you not saying suicidal freak there and again I say you're not funny.' But he laughed as he said it, so surely, he found it funny?

21

'Well, I'm not going to lie and call myself a freak, am I? Remember, I've also been there, attempted that, got the postcard. Fine again I say if you can be suicidal, I can be funny. Wait, I'm confused, why are we repeating ourselves?'

'For shits and giggles?'

'Ugh, why does giggles have to be included? I only want to repeat myself for shits.'

'Sorry, I don't make the rules, you have to include giggles.'

Kat then stubbed out her cigarette.

She didn't answer, she just dramatically crossed her arms in front of herself and made a grumbling noise. Then he did something, it may have been sweet if she didn't already have a boyfriend, but she did have a boyfriend, so it wasn't sweet, it was more like what the actual fuck? Go on, I'll let you guess what he did.

Guessed yet?

He only went and bloody kissed her, on the lips. She was in shock by it, but she was able to breathe a single solitary word out when he pulled away.

'Boyfriend,' was all she was able to say.

'Oh fuck, I'm so sorry, I just thought…Well, I don't know what I thought, I've never seen you with another guy romantically, so I thought you were single, of course, you aren't single, you're far too cool, stupid, stupid me.'

'Different school.'

'I truly am so sorry.'

'No, don't worry, it's fine, you didn't know, no harm no foul.'

'Let's pretend that didn't happen, let me bring this back a few steps, would you like to be my friend instead?'

Kat's laughter returned, 'There was me thinking that goes without saying, given I actually saved your life?'

'OK, maybe you're a little bit funny?'

'I'll take that as an improvement...'

He didn't even get to answer before the door to the roof swung open, a whole five teachers appeared with Juliet.

'Where is he? Is he OK?' One of the teachers asked.

Dominic stood up and said, 'Yeah, I'm fine, thanks to Kat.' Thank God they had stubbed out their cigarettes...No, not thank God Dominic hadn't been injured or you know, died?

Upon seeing Dominic was fine, one of the teachers actually fainted, the teacher who spoke previously said, 'My God, bless Kat.' The other teachers muttered and shook their heads in agreement. 'Would you three like to take the rest of the school day off? I think this situation warrants that...'

'Leave? But I love school?' Kat said as seriously as she could...Which wasn't very seriously at all. But she was successful in stopping herself from laughing.

'No, you can obviously stay if you want, but Dominic, your parents have been called and are coming.'

'Fuck, what was said? What do they know? Tell me.'

'Just what happened I guess. You, roof, wanting to jump.'

'Fuck.'

'Yes, fuck. I wish you the best of luck,' Kat said and hugged him.

'I think I'm going to need it.'

They, all then, walked towards the door and the stairs, but then, when Kat had walked down a whopping three stairs was when she stopped walking and said, 'Actually no, I think it would be best if I go home...'

'That's fine, you can go, that must've been a lot to go through, do you want me to get the counsellor to speak to you?'

'No, I think I'll be fine.' She had to stop herself from laughing, given she had attempted suicide herself, so she didn't see it as quite a big thing as perhaps it was, she was just happy she got to go home early.

'Before we enter the big wide world, set me your digits,' she whispered to Dominic, so they swapped their phones and created themselves as a new contact on each of their phones, Kat even gave her contact a photo, a photo of the back of the teacher's head in front of her, the picture made her laugh.

'Solid, you know you do look like him in a roundabout way…' he whispered to her whilst laughing about the photo.

'No, I don't but I wish I did.'

'OK, fine, you win, I'll put my hands up and say I was wrong,' and he did just that, he raised his arms up in the air and continued laughing, 'maybe you're not a little bit funny, maybe you're quite amusing?'

'Oh, my God. Really? You think that? I think I'm honoured. Just you wait, soon you'll find me hilarious…!'

'I think that might be pushing it just a little…'

They then arrived at reception, where Dominic sat down to wait for his parents, within seconds he pulled out his phone and sent a text to, you guessed it, Kat.

Just mainly checking this is actually your number…But I'm terrified for when they come, take me with you, please?

Kat looked at the text, then had a thought, a devilish little thought, she came up with an evil plan, she could lie.

'My mum is on her way,' lie, 'we live super close,' again lie, 'she's spoken to Dominic's mum,' was she still telling porky pies? 'She's offered to take Dominic home.' Ding, ding, ding, that's a home run of lies.

'Really? OK, fine,' a teacher said.

Before Dominic stood up, he sent a text to Kat.

Bless, if I didn't owe you before, I most definitely owe you now...

Given they were travelling together Kat showed Juliet the texts, she let out a little chuckle which she tried to pass off as a cough and nodded.

'We'll meet my mum on the road, ready?' Kat asked her two friends, to you know, keep up the lie and yes Dominic was now a friend.

'Ready,' Dominic said he couldn't stop himself from smiling.

'Ready,' Juliet said normally.

'Then let's go, I think I see my mum.' She didn't need to lie again, but I guess she was in the swing of it now.

So they left the school reception and left school, as soon as they left and were officially free, all three of them embraced silently and laughed, there was a park nearby, so they decided to go there.

'Nice to meet you, I'm Dominic.' He outstretched his hand to Juliet. She pushed his hand away and hugged him instead.

'I'm Juliet, glad to see you're still alive. Oh fuck, I'm sorry is that insensitive?'

'Who knows? It's a good thing that I don't remotely care…'

They then all walked hand in hand to the park, the park was only about ten minutes away, so it didn't take them long to get there. There was an ice-cream truck parked outside the park. Good place for business, I guess…

'I'm buying, what do you want?' Dominic asked them, he felt like he needed to do something nice for them.

'Aw thank you anything,' Juliet said, so Dominic ordered her the same thing as him.

'Hmm, can I have surf and turf?' Kat asked.

'Oh yeah, sure, it's a new special all ice-cream trucks do…Forget what I said about you being quite amusing…'

'Have I graduated to hilarious yet?'

'Not exactly…'

He also ordered her what he was having, he almost didn't order her anything, but he was too thankful to her to not.

They took their ice-creams from the vendor and went inside the park.

'No, seriously thank you for the ice-cream, I think this is the start of a beautiful friendship,' Kat stated.

'Friendship? Are you definitely happy in your relationship?' How nice! Just forget about Juliet, why don't you?

'It's been two years, so yes, I would say so.'

'Bugger,' Dominic whispered to himself.

'Sorry, what was that?'

'Oh, I said nothing, a fly was just going for my ice-cream, so I swatted it away.'

'Hmm, not sure if I believe you, but OK…'

Chapter 3

Once they were inside the park, they went straight for a stretch of grass and sat in a circle whilst munching on their ice-creams.

'What do you two want to do?' Juliet asked.

'Why do we have to do anything? Why can't we just relax and enjoy our ice-creams? I, for one, am perfectly content,' Kat said and as if to reinforce her point, she laid down on the grass and continued munching on her ice-cream.

'Dominic?' Juliet asked, as if to answer her he also laid down on the grass.

'Note to self, next time don't bother asking them a basic question,' she said and also laid down and they remained like that until they had finished their ice-creams.

When they were finished munching, almost as if she was waiting for them to be done, again Juliet asked, 'What do you two want to do?'

Kat laughed. 'Hey Dominic, can you hear an annoying noise in the background?'

Dominic also laughed. 'Yes, but I think it's happy I'm still alive.'

'Ha, good one,' Kat said and gave him a fist bump.

'You know you can go off some people…' Juliet said.

'For fucks sake, it's that annoying noise again, Dominic, make it stop!'

'Actually, I can help with that.' He went into his bag and pulled out a big pair of headphones. 'They're noise-cancelling.' He passed them to Kat.

'Perfect.'

She put them on her ears and didn't even plug them into anything. Juliet fake zipped her mouth shut.

'Is that better? Have the headphones helped?' Dominic asked.

'Much better, thank you.'

Juliet's lips were now shut, so she just left them sat there where they were and got up to go sit maybe five metres away from them.

'Jules come back, I apologise,' Kat said and actually used her nickname to show she was truly sorry…

Juliet just motioned that her lips were shut, so Kat thought it was best if she stood up and went to go sit down next to her.

'Fine, if you're going to keep up this no talking thing…What can we do? OK, I challenge you to a thumb war. Is madam able to do that?'

Juliet nodded and stretched out her hands for no reason whatsoever other than to thumb war. So, they put their hands together and got down to it, the battle was on. Dominic came over to watch and give some rather questionable commentary.

'Here we have two challengers, who will turn out to be the prince and who will turn out to be the pauper?'

It didn't take Kat long to win, she was rather on the chuffed side. She laughed and made her hand into an L shape and stuck it on her forehead, she then kept repeating the word 'loser,' to Juliet, but Juliet kept the no talking thing up and just turned away.

'Would Mr Commentator like a go?'

'I'm going to give a hesitant yes…'

'OK, fine, come at me, bro.'

So they put their hands together in the thumb wrestle position. There was no commentary coming from Dominic now, he was concentrating too much.

Once again, it didn't take Kat very long to win, she was chuffed.

'OK, so your thumb is not worthy,' she lifted her arm up and bent it in the arm wrestle position, 'What about your arm?'

What with being the man and all, Dominic felt fairly confident in a challenge to an arm wrestle, stupid poor fucker, he only went and bloody lost.

Kat rolled her shoulders backwards with glee, laughed and said, 'Don't hate the player, hate the game.'

'I'll hate who and what I want.'

'As long as it's not me.'

All three of them then laid back down on the grass and relaxed, unspeaking, the wrestling was over, for now…

'Sorry for ruining it, but isn't it so good when you can find people to just share silence with?' Dominic smiled as he said it.

Kat deliberately didn't answer, she just nodded, they were all laid down, so maybe he didn't see it, maybe he did, who knows…She wanted to keep the silence thing up. Then Dominic made the humble mistake of checking his phone.

He had received a text from his mother…

'Fuck, I think I need to go.' He said as he sat up and showed Kat and Juliet the text, they read it and also sat up.

It said *where are you? I'm beyond worried.*

'Fuck, does that mean you have to go?' Kat asked.

'Yes, I think so, unfortunately.'

'Can I help at all?'

'You can text me.'

'Will do, buddy,' Kat pulled Dominic into a big embrace as she said it.

'Good luck,' Juliet said and also hugged him.

So Dominic stood up and without really wanting to, walked away from them, 'Just saying, but I think I should've jumped.' He shouted back to them and laughed.

'What a fucker,' Kat said deliberately quiet enough so he wouldn't hear but Juliet heard and laughed, they both smiled and waved to him as he left. (Smile and wave boys like the penguins from Madagascar, that's a ridiculously specific reference, but there you go…If you don't know it, search it on YouTube…)

When he was gone, when he was out of the picture, Juliet asked because she wanted to know, 'What's the plan?'

'Hmm, I don't really know…I guess…Go home, have lunch, chill out and then get ready for the night ahead?'

'That's a plan I can get behind.'

Upon hearing that, Kat stood up and reached for Juliet's hand, she grabbed it, they stood up together, they went towards the train station and enjoyed a cigarette on the way. The wait for a train wasn't too long when they arrived at the station, so they went down to the platform and waited there.

'I hope Dominic will be fine, about everything,' Juliet stated.

'His head's screwed on right; he'll be fine.'

'But earlier? His head wasn't screwed on right on the roof of the Science Block?'

'He just had a screw loose, it just needed tightening again.'

'Are you a professional screw tightener?'

Kat laughed and said, 'Don't shout it, I'm off the clock.'

So Juliet, instead whispered, 'Are you a professional screw tightener?'

'No, I wouldn't say I'm a professional, I would say it's more recreational. Well, I enjoy it and it pays the bills…'

Juliet laughed at that and that was when the train decided to arrive, so they got on it. Nothing unusual happened on the journey, it was just the usual, typical, to be honest boring ordeal. But they arrived at Kat's house safe and sound, Kat opened her front door and that was that, for now. Journey complete.

Her parents worked together from home, so Kat had to prepare herself for all the questions about how early it was when they went downstairs. They took their shoes off, left their school bags upstairs and went downstairs.

Kat's parents quietened themselves down as the two girls wandered in, they had obviously heard them come in and were talking about it. Kat went over to the fridge and opened it and took a swig of milk from the carton, that was behind her mother, oh yeah, they worked in the Kitchen, perks of working from home, I guess.

'Time?' Kat's father said.

'We know it's early, but don't worry we're not in trouble,' Kat said, hoping to calm them down, they were clearly concerned.

'No, quite the opposite, don't worry,' Juliet said.

'OK, then, by all means, explain,' Kat's father stated.

Juliet was about to tell them the truth because she thought why not? But Kat interrupted her and spoke louder, deliberately.

'We were allowed to come home early because we did really well on a Biology project.' What a lie that was! Kat was worried the truth would instigate a conversation about mental health and because her lack of mental health was a secret, she thought it was best to just avoid that whole topic of conversation.

'Why?' Juliet mouthed to Kat, but Kat pretended she didn't see it, but see it she did, she just chose to ignore it.

'Well, I think I'm ready for lunch, what about you, Jules?'

'Yes, I think so, what do you want?'

'I don't know, I suppose heating up a tin of soup is easy?'

'I'm no Jamie Oliver, but I think I can do that…'

So they walked to the pantry, which was just outside of the Kitchen, where the family's various canned goods were kept. Kat quickly picked some tomato soup and went to leave the pantry, but Juliet stopped her.

'Why are we living in secret? Also Biology? You know I'm shit at Biology.'

'Doesn't matter, I just didn't fancy being questioned and anyway it's Dominic's life, he doesn't even know my parents, so it's not exactly fair to share something ridiculously personal about him, is it? I don't think you can get more personal.'

'OK, fair,' Juliet said and grabbed one of the two tins of soup that Kat was holding, 'Now, let's heat these up, I'm starving.'

Thank God, that was too close for comfort, was all Kat could think. So she followed Juliet out of the Pantry and back to the Kitchen, where they made their soup, it only took minutes for them to heat them up in the microwave.

They ate whilst playing on their phones, at the Kitchen table where Kat's parents were working, when Kat received two texts, one from her boyfriend and one from Dominic. HMM, TOGETHER? COINCIDENCE…? I THINK NOT…

The one from her boyfriend was boring, it just said *how are you?* Yawn. She didn't reply, she would do it later.

But Dominic said *seriously thank you for everything today, when I say you saved my life, I'm not even joking.*

It didn't take Kat long to think of a response to send, so she replied very soon after she read it by saying *no, don't thank me, I just know how hard life can be sometimes ha it almost makes you want to jump off a building. Am I right?*

He replied in seconds by letting her know *I think your sense of humour needs to be medically sectioned.*

This made Kat chuckle. *Really? Just my sense of humour and not all of me? Sorry, serious talk now…But how are home and parents?*

Shit was all he said.

Can I help? Kat genuinely wanted to help.

You can kill me.

Sorry, I'm kind of having a save people kind of day rather than killing them…

33

Bugger, was all he said, so she laughed, put her phone down and finished munching on her soup, Juliet was already finished because she hadn't been texting, so she put her dirty bowl by the sink. It didn't take Kat very long to finish her soup after Juliet, but when she did she also put her dirty utensils by the sink. They then had a post-meal smoke, inside, in the Kitchen because it was obviously allowed because that was where Kat's parents smoked.

'Upstairs?' Kat asked when their cigarettes were finished.

'Sure,' Juliet answered.

They quickly went upstairs. When they entered Kat's room, Juliet said, 'I think it's now time for part three of the plan, arguably my favourite part, but chill out.'

'Agreed, chill out how?'

'Film or games and music.'

'I think I vote film. I'm not tired but I don't want to have to move or think, big morning…'

'OK, true, do you want to talk about it?'

'There's nothing to say and besides you already know what happened.' Kat laughed. 'We did a really good Biology project.'

But Juliet didn't laugh. 'Why do I feel you're not telling me everything?' Because she wasn't, go on, keep going…

'But obviously, I am?'

'OK, true, I believe you.' But you shouldn't believe her, she's a little liar…Or quite a big liar…

'Good, glad that's sorted, now what film?'

'Hmm, I don't know, I don't know, is it early enough for a *Lord of the Rings* marathon?'

'OK, so I'll take that as a fuck off to watching some light comedy?'

Juliet just laughed.

'Given we're going out tonight, I'd say we have time for the first two,' Kat answered properly this time, but she took all three film cases off her shelf, just in case and Juliet put the TV on and then sat on the sofa in front of it. In seconds Kat joined her, put the first DVD in the player and also sat down.

During the first film, Kat may have fallen asleep. Aw, how sweet!

Chapter 4

Kat was able to wake herself up whilst Juliet was putting on the second film, so I guess she didn't wake herself up at all, she was woken up.

'Sorry, I tried to be quiet, so as not to wake you, you looked so cosy! Do you feel rested? Was it a good sleep?'

'Ah fuck, did the fellowship break without me?' (*Lord of the Rings* joke, you either get it or you don't…)

'I'm afraid so, but we're about to see two almighty towers being built, so at least you haven't missed that, it could be worse…' (Again, *Lord of the Rings* joke, are they nerds? Or are they NERDS?)

Kat actually successfully watched the second film, she stayed awake for the entirety, her previous nap was needed.

Lord, they were long films, when the second film finished, they saw it as time to get ready for the night ahead, so Kat stood up and went to put a CD on.

Kat then thought she should reply to her boyfriend's text, it wasn't exactly a deep conversation, so it was easy enough to do.

I'm fine, going out tonight so just about to start getting ready. Was her reply, she wasn't going to send a text about the reality of her day.

He replied instantly, *OK, have fun, don't do anything I wouldn't do.*

Kat didn't reply, but she laughed, don't do anything he wouldn't do? So, no drug, ever?

The two girls then got themselves ready, slowly but surely, Kat only had one mirror, so they took it in turns to use it and do their make-up.

It was Kat's turn to get dressed first, while Juliet used the mirror and did her make-up, so Kat looked through her wardrobe, but no garments took her fancy, then she had an idea. The most brilliant idea!

So, she walked to the other end of her room, where she kept her Halloween costumes, it was mid-October so even though it was the same month as Halloween, wearing a costume this early on was bizarre. But did Kat care? No, not in the slightest. She started to rummage through them until she found something she thought was acceptable.

Kat laughed, 'OK, I think I now know what I'm going to wear, so Juliet please close your eyes, let me show you.'

So, Juliet did just that while Kat ran over to the mirror, drew a big black lightning bolt on her face and put the Hogwarts cloak she had found on her body. Bonus, it was also something that covered her wrist, so it had its uses…

Kat started singing *The Harry Potter* Puppet Pals. (If you don't know it again look it up on YouTube…)

'I'm Harry Potter, Harry Harry Potter.' Kat's singing inspired Juliet to open her eyes. (Again, The Harry Potter Puppet Pals.)

Upon looking at Kat, all Juliet could say was, 'Oh fuck, really?'

'You better believe it. Haza Pots is ready to parrrrrdy.'

'Do what you want I guess, but there is no way I am going as Ron.'

'Ugh, OK fine, you're no fun, what about Hermione?'

'What about Juliet?'

Kat started laughing, 'But I'm Harry Potter, not Romeo?'

'You can fuck right off.' The amount of Romeo and Juliet gags she had heard in her life was ridiculous.

Juliet had finished with her make-up, so decided to get dressed into something more normal than her best friend, she brought a skirt and a top with her from home, so she put them on. There was no way in Hell she was going as Ron or Hermione.

'You look lovely this evening, shame not as good as me…' Kat said, well, Harry Potter said and started twerking.

'Just so you know you're driving me to drugs, can I have a line?' Juliet asked.

'Does that mean you don't want dinner?' Kat enquired.

'Nah, I'll be fine without, food always makes me feel gross if I eat it just before going out, remember Sandra's party?'

'The party not so much, but the fact you became a little throwing-up demon, yes.'

'Well, then there you go.'

'Ha, well, OK then, yeah sure,' she passed Juliet her drug tin, 'but shall we wait until we're there to pop the pills?'

'Probably wise,' Juliet said as she racked herself up a line, she snorted it easily, she had done it before and passed it over to Kat. Kat did the same, nice and smooth and exhaled.

'That shit ain't bad, definitely worth the money…' Kat said as she wiped her nose, 'hopefully, the pills are good too.'

'Yes, hopefully, I love how it's easier for someone who's under the age of eighteen to acquire something illegal of the drug variety than to just get booze…How long is our journey?'

Maybe it was because Juliet was expecting the answer to be a very long amount of time, so it would be an even longer amount of time before she got another hit or maybe she just wanted another hit. But make and snort another hit she did.

Kat wasn't sure, so she checked Journey Planner on her phone.

'Not too bad, about half an hour.' Kat also prepared and snorted another line, but solely because Juliet did.

'OK, so shall we go?'

'Roger, roger,' Kat said and pretended to be a droid from *Star Wars*, it didn't really work with the whole *Harry Potter* get up, but let her do her, I guess…

'What do we need to take?' Juliet asked.

'You know what, I don't know the Kitchen sink.'

'You're not funny. Go on, guess who that comment reminded Kat of, talk about her humour.' So, she checked her phone.

He had texted her again, *my parents are making this so much harder than this needs to be, sorry for bothering you on your Friday night.* George Clooney said, 'OK fine, not George Clooney, but it could've been. OK, no it couldn't…It was Dominic.

No apology necessary talk away, I'm going out to a little get-together tonight, want me to see if I can get you invited? Was Kat's reply.

Really? You'd do that for me? Shame, there's no way in hell my parents will let me out because I'd love to see you.

To mimic him from earlier, her reply was one word and one word only *bugger* was all she said. 'OK, so what do we need to take?' It was Kat who asked this time, Juliet answered more seriously than Kat...

No Kitchen sinks were mentioned. But surely the Kitchen sink was needed?

'Travel pass? Drugs? And I don't know a water bottle?'

'The holy trinity?'

'Amen.' Juliet made sure she had another holy trinity, well, the holy pair, her travel pass was downstairs by the front door where Kat's was.

To that, Kat made a crucifix with her fingers, as if warding off a vampire and pointed it at Juliet because she had said holy trinity.

'Ready Dracula?' Kat asked.

'Steady,' Juliet said.

'Go?'

'Indeed.'

They walked to Kat's door arm in arm and went down the stairs.

'OK, I think we just need shoes,' Kat said, it wasn't cold enough for coats.

So, Kat put on some trainers, whereas Juliet put on her school shoes, they shared the mindset that high heels were so uncomfortable, so why wear them?

'Ready?' They grabbed their travel passes.

'I think so,' but then Kat started laughing, 'but wait? Where's my wand?'

'It's where you left it I'm pretty sure. Up your ass?'

'Oh yes, so it is.'

Kat shouted a goodbye downstairs to her parents, the girls were now fully ready, so they left the house and walked to the train station, which wasn't very far away from Kat's house, about a cigarette away, so they had one.

The journey was uneventful but they arrived at Ryan's house safely, there was a short walk in between the station and his house, so they each smoked a cigarette while walking. When they were outside his house, was when they decided to pop the pills, the real reason they brought the water bottle. They weren't just keen to keep hydrated.

'Ready?' Juliet asked, but Kat took that as a statement rather than a question, so she rang the doorbell.

Ryan was the one who opened the door.

'Why, hello there,' Ryan said and outstretched his hands.

'We've brought the parrrrttty,' Kat said.

'Oh, but I thought you were the party?'

'Yes, we are and we brought ourselves?'

'Good. Come on, get in here!'

There was music playing, thank God, so they danced their way inside.

'Have you guys popped a pill?'

'Literally seconds ago.'

'Fuck, that's perfect, so have we.'

'We? But I only see you? I know this is supposed to be a small party, but jeez…'

It was at that moment Ryan opened the door to the garden outside to reveal maybe ten other guests, Kat and Juliet knew them and got on fairly well with them all but they weren't all ridiculously close buddies. They all sat down.

'What do you want to do?' Ryan asked.

'I have a really weird request. But can we by any chance play Twister? I've always wanted to play it whilst on pills,' Kat said.

'Twister? But I'm uncoordinated as fuck. Anyways, no you got it all wrong, Harry Potter performs magic, he doesn't move his body magically?' A boy who Kat knew as Eric said.

'Just think, with pills, that will make it even better and Harry Potter does what he wants, my scar proves it.' Kat pointed to the lightning bolt on her forehead.

Eric laughed.

'That's a possible plan, we have Twister,' Ryan said.

'No, wrong word, that's a definite plan.'

'I'll play,' a girl, I think it was Leah, said.

The others nodded.

'But aren't we too many people to play Twister?' Eric said, to say he felt happy by this realisation, was an understatement and a half.

'Oh fuck, yes, good point,' Juliet said.

'For fucks sake it sucks having too many friends!' Kat said sweetly because they weren't really her friends, just her acquaintances.

'But in all seriousness, do you guys want to do anything? Or just chill out here?' the good little host enquired.

'Well, I don't know about you, but I think I want a line,' Kat said.

Juliet shook her head in agreement, that was all the agreement Kat needed, so Kat prepared and they both snorted a line.

The rest of the evening was fairly relaxed, well as relaxed as it could be on MDMA and cocaine, well, it was a party after all…Kat even played a game of Twister with the allegedly uncoordinated Eric, shock horror he won, but I suppose Twister doesn't really need immense levels of coordination or maybe Kat was just immensely shit at it?

The evening was good all in all.

The evening finished with Kat and Eric sat outside having a cigarette in the garden whilst Kat was waiting for a taxi to take her home, she was now going home alone because Juliet was now upstairs getting frisky with Ryan.

'Those kids are so crazy ahaha,' Eric laughed as he said it. 'There was me thinking he liked you? Obviously not, sorry…'

'Ha, no, I'm taken. I think he knows that.'

'WELL, I HOPE THEY'RE HAVING FUN,' Eric shouted up.

'Well, it's whatever makes them happy,' was Kat's answer.

'It's all about other people's happiness with you, isn't it?'

'Well, I care about other people's happiness.'

'What about yours?'

'OK, well, I'm miserable about the fact you won Twister…'

'Ahaha, don't hate the player, hate the game.'

'Oh, come off it.' She hit him on the shoulder, then checked her phone, taxi had arrived, it was time to vacate the premises and go home for Kat.

'You OK?' Eric asked.

'Yeah, yeah, my taxi has just arrived.'

'Aw, does that mean you have to leave?'

'I think that's how taxis work.'

Eric laughed. 'Wow, so you're funny as well?'

OK, that proved it, any mention of her humour made her think of him, that kid she met earlier, so she checked her phone.

He hadn't texted her, so she texted him. Well, I suppose there's not really much to say in a reply to the word bugger.

Close to school kind of, taken a pill but it's worn off, about to get in the taxi, you can't go to the party, but shall I bring the party to you and come over? Was what she said to Dominic.

He replied almost instantly, well, in a couple of minutes, *I fucking wish, but I actually think there's a good chance, especially because it's so late, my parents won't let you in.*

How rude. But I saved their darling son's life?

At this point, I kind of wish you didn't...

No, don't you fucking dare say anything like that to me again. Trust me, I know it's hard, I KNOW, been there tried that. Pick someone else to read your pity party, not me.

She put her phone away, hugged Eric and went back into the house and said goodbye to the remaining guests, well, apart from the host and her best friend. She left the house, saw her taxi, went over to the road and clambered into it.

Her destination hadn't changed so the driver knew where she was going, so nothing needed to be said. So, she checked her phone, she had received a text, I'm not even going to say who from, but it said *OK, I'm sorry, forgive me for not being completely normal the day of...*

Kat inhaled and exhaled deeply, she thought about her reply before she pressed send on it, she wanted to make it good, so she eventually settled on:

I'm not expecting normality, I'm aware this whole situation is fucked, but don't tell me, the girl who saved you, that you wish I didn't.

OK, fair, I'm sorry.

So Kat leaned back in the car and stared out the window, the journey didn't feel too long, even though Ryan wasn't exactly her next-door neighbour. But she got to her home, alive and not in a body bag.

'Cheers,' she said to the driver, got out of the car and waved.

She walked up the steps to her house, unlocked the door and went inside. It wasn't exactly early but of course her parents were still awake, all the lights were still on. They were most likely downstairs watching TV, but I thought they worked downstairs? Open plan Living Room and Kitchen, they work all day in the Kitchen, then walk a few metres and watch TV all evening in the Living Room. Can't be bad! A five-metre commute!

Kat couldn't be bothered to go downstairs and see her parents; there would no doubt be a conversation about the location of Juliet and Kat just couldn't be asked about that at that moment in time.

So, she shouted down the stairs, 'Party good, but tiring, going to bed, night.'

'OK darling, I hope you sleep well and we'll see you tomorrow,' her mother shouted back.

So, Kat went upstairs, brushed her pearly whites in the bathroom and then went all the way upstairs to her room where she peacefully tried to fall asleep immediately.

Oh no, wait, no she didn't, that must've been a different Kat…My bad…She only went and took off her Hogwarts cloak, she didn't put it away, she left it out because she had decided she would wear it tomorrow at her dad's fortieth birthday party, she was a witch, it was necessary to wear it and then, to round off the day, she cut her wrist, the cutting had become a routine, it was addictive.

Don't ask me how, I'm no doctor, just a narrator. She went harder tonight, probably because she had been out and actually had a nice time. She actually started crying, no, not because of the physical pain but because of the mental pain. She couldn't help but admire Dominic for his idea, jumping off a building may take balls, but it was fool-proof, whereas taking a whole bunch of drugs, not so much…

Chapter 5

When she awoke it was daylight outside, so the next day, thank God. The first thing she did was check the time on her phone, it was half past ten, time to get up! So, get up she did! But first, check texts…

Her boyfriend had texted her minutes ago *in car, on the way!* Thank God was all she thought. She did love him, he was odd, but so was she, all be it in a completely different way, but hey, that was young love.

So, Kat replied with a *sweet! Can't wait to see you my g.*

He replied in seconds, I guess there's not much else to do whilst sat in a car…

Who the fuck is g? Sounds kind of similar, but I'm b, he said because his name was Ben, but either way quite a terrible joke…

Kat didn't reply to that, she would see him soon enough anyway, so there was no need. She stood up from lying in bed, put her phone in her pocket, put her Hogwarts cloak back on and drew a black lightning bolt on her forehead, just like yesterday…She was tempted to do it in pen rather than make-up but she did it in black eye-liner. She now felt ready to face the day, so she went down the stairs.

When she arrived down the stairs the first thing she noticed was that her parents weren't down there, *they must be dead*, Kat thought to herself. OK, that may be a little lie, she didn't think that instead she thought *they must be asleep.* But that was useful, let them sleep! It would mean no talk about Juliet.

So she went to go get herself some breakfast, just some humble cereal again today, minimal effort was needed for toast, but it was still too much effort and so she sat down on the sofa, put the TV on and watched it. A TV breakfast, how sweet!

So she watched some Saturday morning dribble, ate her bowl of cereal and had a cigarette. In about an hour her parents came downstairs and joined Kat, did they get themselves any breakfast? No, did they fuck, like usual they just heated themselves up a mug of coffee each in the microwave. How nutritious! They also had a cigarette. Again how nutritious!

Kat's father then motioned for her to give him the TV remote because why use words? He, like usual, put the news on and didn't even watch it, he just played a game on his phone, I guess having the remote for the TV was more of a control thing for him. It was his TV technically, his argument would be *well, I paid for it.* Man owns TV, man controls TV.

'Plan of action?' Kat asked.

'Well, I guess you and your mother will clean the house soon for later.' No, he didn't just say that because it was for his birthday party, so he shouldn't have to clean, he really was that much of a male chauvinist.

When Kat's mother was finished with her cigarette, she took a big gulp of coffee and asked her daughter, 'Are you ready? Also, why on earth are you wearing that?'

'Ready? For what? Sitting here relaxing? About my outfit, it may be the weekend, but I just love school!'

'Ha, I forgot you were funny.' He only went a bloody said it, the f word, no not forgot. I'm not going to spell it out for you...

But she checked her phone to see if Dominic had texted her, he hadn't, so she wondered if should she text him. But decided against it. It was weird to continually text a younger guy when she had a boyfriend already, so what if some of their problems were similar? It was weird and they had only met yesterday?

'So, cleaning?' Kat enquired.

'Yes, you dust and polish? I'll hoover?' So that's how they started, Kat even took off her Hogwarts cloak, so as not to get it dirty, whilst the father watched TV, as per. Cleaning also took place upstairs, where guests would also be that evening, Kat also made a big triangle out of wine glasses, for guests to select later.

When the cleaning was completed as good as it was going to be, Kat and her mother went back downstairs to have a cigarette. The father had now fully stopped playing games on his phone and was fully watching TV, not flicking through both.

As soon as Kat had finished her cigarette and stubbed it out, she put her Hogwarts cloak back on and then the doorbell decided to ring, was that perfect timing? Or was it perfect timing? Given it was most likely her boyfriend and he didn't smoke, I'm going to say perfect timing. So, she went upstairs to open the front door, it was obviously her boyfriend and his family.

'No, no, no, the party isn't for hours yet, go home!' Kat shouted to them.

'Come here, you're lucky I love you,' Ben said, as he hugged and gave her a little kiss on the cheek. 'Harry.'

Her answer was a smile.

They clambered into the house, with all their stuff and went up to the spare room, to put it there, where they would be sleeping, yes, all of them, Ben included. Kat's parents didn't know Kat and Ben had slept together, so the thought of them sharing a bed was abhorrent.

It didn't take them very long to get settled, they had done this before. Kat waited by the front door for her boyfriend, his parents went all the way downstairs to Kat's parents, but he stayed by Kat and he said nothing and just started kissing her.

The kissing took them to the upstairs Living Room which had two sofas, so Kat let herself be pushed down onto one, the kissing got more intense. He wanted her, no he needed her. Of course, they ended up sleeping together, what a good welcome! Kat should welcome all people into her home like that, with her body…

When they were all finished and it was all said and done, they straightened up their clothes onto their bodies, no, they didn't even take them off, just in case a parent came up the stairs. Not exactly the definition of romance, is it? Kat didn't even take off her Hogwarts outfit, so it was an age-rated Harry Potter film, Harry Potter and the Chamber of Penis.

Then the kids went down the stairs to the parents, it was still early, but they had already started drinking together.

'Oh, has the train to party central already arrived here?' Kat asked because even she thought it was a little early to start drinking.

Ben's mother raised up her glass and borderline shouted, 'choo-choo.' She didn't really pass as a train, but she tried…

'Well, if you can't beat them, join them I guess…' So, Ben helped her pour two gin and tonics, when they were made, Kat took a deep swig.

Then her mother, maybe stupidly, asked her, 'So, do you know what you're wearing tonight? Are you wearing a dress?'

She thought to herself, *do I lie or tell the truth?* Kat thought the truth would mean her mum would make her get changed and mark my words, she would be Harry Potter tonight, come hell or high water, so she lied.

'Yeah, a dress I think.' Saying I think it was crucial, so it wasn't technically a lie, she may as well have said, "Yeah, I may wear a dress I think, but that's not really allowed, it's not exactly school uniform, is it? I'll just wear my cloak."

What shall we do? Kat wondered.

'I don't think it's quite late enough to get ready yet, so game?' Kat's mother said.

Kat nodded and found and brought the one game they had which she knew could be played with six people, Strip Poker! OK, not Strip Poker, regular Poker…

She put it on the Kitchen table, it was clear of anything work-related, her parents had cleared all their work stuff off it earlier. So Kat sat down and measured out chips for everyone, they all gravitated towards the table and sat down, Kat gave them all their chips and grabbed the cards and dealt.

That was the joy of Poker, you could play a game for hours, given you didn't play stupidly. But when Kat's mother lost was when she decided to say, 'OK, I think it might be time to get ready for tonight.'

Get ready? But I am ready? Do you mean relax on my laptop? Well, don't mind if I do...Kat made herself laugh at that thought because her plan was to pretend getting ready until after the first guest arrived so her mother couldn't force her to get changed, well, she hoped that would be the case...

She went upstairs to her room, checked and added to her make-up, well, her lightning bolt and went to go lay in bed, on her laptop. She mainly just listened to music, until she thought it was late enough to grace downstairs with her presence. Some guests had arrived.

Her boyfriend started laughing and went over and whispered to her 'ha! Knew you wouldn't get changed!'

'I was worried that if I got changed, Voldemort would come and get me, it's no laughing matter...I could've died...'

'Oh God, of course not.' He tried and failed to be serious, 'but he didn't. Thank God. You're here! He didn't get you!'

'I wouldn't say thank God for being at my dad's birthday party...'

'Well, I would, free booze.' He was now onto wine, so he took a deep swig.

'Oh, you're now onto wine? You put the ass in class.' She laughed and also got herself a glass of wine and practically downed it and got herself another, 'OK, I think I'm ready.'

'Jeez, shall I just get you the bottle and a straw?'

'You know what, yes please...'

'I was joking...'

'I wasn't...'

Kat's mother then came over to her and angrily pointed and gestured at what she was wearing, she was beyond pissed off. 'You lied, you said dress, why?'

'I've literally just explained to Ben why, do I have to explain again? Really?' Her mother just nodded.

'OK fine, are you listening?' Kat started laughing and so did Ben. 'I was worried that if I got changed Voldemort would come and get me.'

'For fucks sake, having so many people over is stressful enough, why can't you just act normal for once?'

'B-b-b-but I'm not normal? I'm a wizard.'

'I can't be dealing with you, just go and hand these out.' Her mother handed her a platter of shop-bought sausage rolls. Kat did as she was told.

More people arrived, most people gravitated to the upstairs area by the front door because there was a snooker table there, where people played pool. Games were constant, but just because it was her table doesn't mean Kat was any good, ha she was awful.

By now, her mother had calmed down, probably because she had drunk rather a lot. Her father was happy and having a good time, I mean all his friends had gathered to celebrate him, I don't think it was possible to be miserable in that situation.

'Can we please go somewhere more private? With no people?' Kat's dad's friend asked the birthday boy.

'Oh, um, yeah sure, is my room, OK?'

'Sounds perfect.'

So, they went upstairs to his room because his friend needed privacy to have a nap. OK, no he didn't, that's a lie…

'Do you have a little mirror?' he asked the father when they had got up there, to his room. Ah, OK, he wanted to do his make-up, makes sense…Nope, OK, lie again…

But the father found a little mirror amongst some of the mother's eye shadow.

The father had a good idea of what was going on, he wasn't born yesterday.

'Happy birthday!' the friend said and pulled out a little baggie full of white powder.

'Thought so.' The father said, 'God, it's been years. Let it snow?'

'Well, the weather outside is frightful?'

The father then began racking himself up a line. It may have been years, but old habits die hard or they don't die at all, there was a finesse in the way he did it.

'I'm pretty sure if I take this I'll only want more, so give me your dealer's number?' the father asked his friend.

'Yeah, sure, you've already met him, he works for me.'

They both took their phones out and exchanged his number.

'Ha, not going to lie you'd kind of expect that from Gareth,' the father said because the friend only had one employee.

'What can I say? He's a delivery driver through and through, he delivers wine for me by day and drugs by night. Boy, do I know how to pick them.'

The friend then took out a banknote, rolled it up and gave it to the father. Was he ready? No, not really. Did that matter? No, not really.

Was he going to snort the line he had made? You can bet your bottom dollar he was.

He then took it. My God, he forgot how good it was.

'That's decent, I could do that again.' Wait, I'm getting a transmission from the future, he does do it again! Many, many times…

The joys of being a third-person narrator is I can go here, there and anywhere.

The friend then took a line, there was some residue left on the glass, so the father used his finger to put it on his gums. Just like old times…With that whole having a daughter malarkey it had been years.

'I really appreciate you giving me that by the way.'

'No worries, let's do another and then go and enjoy your party.'

'OK, it's not like you need to convince me…' the father said as he racked himself up another line, he took it and then passed the mirror back to his friend. Who did the same. The father then fully cleaned up the mirror with his finger and put the residue on his gums, it was all nice and clean now, no residue anymore. The father then put the now clean mirror in a drawer in his bedside table, hmm was he planning on using it again? HMM?

'Downstairs, party, ready?' the friend asked.

'I'm ready for anything!' I think the father could feel it.

And that was that. Drugs taken; they re-joined the party again. Kat definitely seemed more drunk than earlier, she couldn't even walk straight, she was trying to play pool, oh how she tried, but it had all gone to shit.

'Can I have a game with my daughter please?'

It was his friend playing her, so an adult. 'Yeah, sure but good luck, she's gone.'

'I think I'll be able to handle her.' But he wasn't, by the third move she had disappeared, she had gone downstairs, ate some leftover sausage rolls that were in the fridge and passed out on the Living Room sofa where she had started her day.

Ben had actually made it to bed, he was drunk but Kat was on a whole other level.

Ben…drunk. Kat…pissed.

It was late, so guests started leaving and going home. All in all, it was a good evening, the father even reconnected with an old, white flame.

Chapter 6

It was the morning after the night before. Kat woke up on the downstairs sofa, that was weird, she couldn't remember getting there. In fact, there was a lot she couldn't remember, *oh fuck* she thought to herself, *did I get drunk? Or did I get drunk?*

I think you got drunk...

Her boyfriend and his family then came down the stairs, but not her parents, how odd. *Hmm maybe they were up ridiculously late snorting lines of blow and that's why they weren't up yet,* Kat thought to herself, oh no, wait, no she didn't. The thought of that was so ridiculous to her, that it wasn't even a thought, but truth hurts...

'Breakfast?' Ben's mother asked as she entered the Kitchen slash Living Room, 'and how is the little munchkin's head this morning?'

'Yes, to breakfast, sustenance is needed.' She then started laughing, stood up and went over to put her hands around her boyfriend. 'I just need some h to the o and something greasy, if I don't get it, I may die...'

'Well then, what the lady wants, the lady shall get,' the boyfriend said and laughed. 'Now sit down, I'll cook.'

'Appreciated,' and Kat did as she was told like a good little girl and sat down.

Ben found some eggs in the fridge and started frying them, but only for Kat, his parents were quite capable of getting their own breakfast, was his thought process. He dished everything up on a plate, gave it to Kat and sat down next to her on the sofa.

'Where's ours?' his mother asked and motioned to the father.

'I think you're quite capable of cooking yourselves an egg. Kat's not very well, she's quite warm, I think she has a temperature…' He put a hand on her forehead as if checking her temperature. She just kissed him when he said that, no she wasn't very well…

'Charming,' his mother scoffed.

But he ignored her and instead watched Kat eat, her investment into the food showed him just how thankful she was, she scoffed it.

She finished her food rather quickly, put her plate on the floor and put her arms around her boyfriend, to show him how thankful she was. His mother begrudgingly made some breakfast for herself and her husband, so Kat put on the TV and her boyfriend put his arms around her. She then rolled herself a cigarette and had it, it wasn't that he didn't know she smoked, it's just that he didn't smoke himself so she didn't like to do it in front of him, but she had just eaten, so smoke time!

She stuck on a film she had heard about but never seen. It was decent, but within minutes after it finished her parents decided to get up and came down the stairs. The father made a b-line for his usual armchair, he didn't even need to move for his remote, the film was finished, so the daughter just threw it at him.

He rolled himself a cigarette, smoked it and stuck his eyes onto the TV. Whereas the mother was up and about in the Kitchen, her first task was to put the oven on, her second task was of course heat up two mugs of coffee in the microwave, as that was happening and heat was being applied to the coffee, she put a tray of bacon in the oven. As Ben's parents were sitting on her armchair, she picked up her cigarettes and joined the two kids on the sofa and brought the two coffees over as she did so. When she was all settled, she said the word 'morning,' to everyone.

Kat laughed. 'No, try again…'

The mother looked concerned, 'Um, merry Christmas?'

Kat kept her laughter going, Ben also joined in with the laughter. 'How can that be your first response to no, try again?'

Kat's laughter became louder, she just couldn't stop herself, 'Try looking at the cock?'

'I'm sorry, what?'

Ben couldn't stop himself from grinning, his laughter also increased and then he borderline shouted the word 'clock!'

'Oh sorry, I must've misheard you…' the mother said and looked at the clock.

'Except, no you didn't…' Kat whispered to her boyfriend and leaned back as she said it to try and make noise, to try and drown out the sound of her voice, but not his voice because he carried on laughing.

'Wait, why am I looking at the clock? I'm lost.'

Even the father put his head in his hands at that, Kat then laughed at her idea of a response, so she saluted and said in as much of an Irish accent as she could, 'Top of the morning to ya.'

'But it's not morning anymore? OK, I'm with you…'

'Are you sure you're sure? Because that was borderline painful…' Kat said, she had been able to control herself and stop laughing…

'Are you unnecessary or I don't know, not necessary?' was the mother's response she also put her head in her hands.

'No, I'm Kat, you should really know, you were involved in the whole naming process of me…Weren't you?'

'Don't remind me.'

'Don't remind you about the best day of your life?'

'I don't think you can call it that somehow…I think ouch is a better descriptor…My God, did you hurt…'

'Ouch? I hurt you?' Kat again laughed at her response before she said it, 'Wait, are you saying childbirth hurts?'

The mother didn't even grace that with a response, but everyone else laughed, instead of replying the mother stood up, walked over to the oven and checked on the bacon.

'Will there be enough for yours truly?' Ben asked, he now decided he was hungry and why cook for yourself when someone else can cook for you?

'Yes, of course, Ben, but have you guys not had breakfast?'

'No, don't worry, only me.' Kat said, 'He cooked but didn't eat.'

'No, no way, I'm not having this…' his mother said.

'I know, I know, aren't I smart? I impress myself with my brain power sometimes…' he whispered to Kat and swished his shoulders (ha Swish Swish, song by Katy Perry, if you don't know it, I give up…Listen to it…)

'I think the food should be ready in approximately ten,' Kat's mother said and Kat just laughed away. When it was ready Kat's mother dished it up and the two guys helped, well, they dished up theirs…

From ages ago Ben finally replied to his mother with a 'You know, I don't understand why you're not having any of this, shame because it smells so very good.' As if to prove his point he moved his nose along his sandwich and inhaled as if it were cocaine. No, no, steady on, she wasn't dating her dad…

When he had finished his sandwich he said to Kat, 'Would you like to go upstairs and play pool?' But she knew that as *would you like to go upstairs and have sex?* Who said romance was dead? It was just getting raunchy.

'Yeah, but beware, I'll win.'

I don't think you can really win sex, it wasn't like he was going to rape her which would be losing at sex for her, winning for him, so her statement was just a lie (BUT SPOILER ALERT he does actually do that in the future…).

But they went upstairs and got jiggy with it, you know, down with the kids, where they had and in the same way as the day before, when he finished because she never did, they decided to actually play pool…

Eventually, at long last, Ben's parents came up the stairs, it was time for them to leave and go home now. So they grabbed their stuff from the upstairs spare room in which they slept and left Kat's home and started the merry drive back to their humble abode. Kat's parents also came up the stairs to wish them goodbye.

'Thank you so much, for everything!' Ben's mother shouted from the car, Kat and her family waved them goodbye and they drove off. That was that social interaction done for the day, well, it was probably done for weeks, yes you heard me, weeks for the star-crossed lovers.

Kat and her parents then stopped waving at them because they were then gone, driven off into the distance...

'OK, so plan?' the mother asked.

'Well, I'm guessing you crazy kids will go downstairs and watch TV, whereas little old me, is going to do my homework in my room.'

'How exciting! OK, have fun!' Yes, because all teenagers have fun doing homework. I swear the definition of homework is fun?

Kat didn't even say anything to that, what response could she even give? She just went up the stairs to her room, she wanted to be alone, well away from her parents, she was a grungy teenager after all. When she arrived at her room, she immediately grabbed her laptop to do some homework on it! Oh no, wait, no she didn't, she did grab her laptop straight away though, but going on the internet was far more interesting than doing homework.

Her phone then jingled to signify she had received a text. *Look I said I was sorry, what more can I say? I like talking to you, so maybe...Talk to me?* Do I even need to say who sent that? Go on, guess...

No, my bad completely, I was busy, sorry, can't spend all day on my phone when you have guests. She made herself laugh at the last part of her message *I have a life* was the last part of her message.

He took a while to respond, maybe half an hour? So Kat started writing her essay for school, it wasn't exactly easy, like it took time, but it had to be done. But then her phone buzzed, it said *a life? But there was me thinking you wanted death?* So, she stopped writing, the essay could and would be done later and, instead, poured her focus onto her phone only. She laughed at his reply, but mainly at hers.

Life? Death? The point is I was busy...getting the d...

You cheeky minx! Sorry for making this fun conversation serious, but I'm scared, my parents have decided to send me to therapy. I'm terrified.

Upon reading this Kat actually said 'fuck,' out loud, she couldn't imagine anything worse, but no, she had to put her make Dominic feel better hat on. But she couldn't, she just couldn't. So, she texted the same thing she had said, no, not that she was sure therapy would be fun, she didn't even say that? All she messaged was *fuck.*

He replied quick enough with an *oh, gee thanks, for making me feel better, helpful, really helpful...Fuck? Wow, you really are happy for me...*

You're welcome, but fuck. Was all she could message him. Worried was the wrong word to describe what she felt for him, but if she was sent to therapy, that would be it, she'd be gone, out of there, dead. Finished. Complete. Goodbye, Elvis has left the building.

This is not a situation where I should be trying to make you feel better, but I'm sure it'll be fine, what's the worst that could happen? Will it make me want to die? Oh no, wrong word oops, I do want to die...Will it make me want to live? Kat found his reply funny, so she laughed, but then calmed herself down in order to respond to him.

Yeah, OK, very good, but it could change who you are. And I don't want that, she said seriously, all traces of humour gone.

Is that you saying you like me? Even Kat could feel his excitement in his question. Aw, he had a smidgen of a crush…

As a friend, yes. Way to kill his excitement. She killed it so much that he didn't reply again, so that was that conversation over, for now.

After waiting a few minutes for the reply that wasn't coming, she returned to her essay on her laptop. While she was doing it her boyfriend texted, but upon seeing it was him she didn't reply.

Bit weird, but OK, reply straightaway to a guy you barely know, but not your boyfriend, OK? When the essay was finished, she was just happy it was over, so she emailed it to her teacher and put on some music. It wasn't even like she had finished all her homework, but that essay had been hanging over her head, like a helmet, that instead of protecting your head it decided to hit you, repeatedly.

She thought, after completing her essay and starting more homework, that she deserved an actual break. A break involving smoke, so she went downstairs because smoking wasn't allowed in her room, well smoking wasn't allowed upstairs full stop. So, she went downstairs, upon getting down there, she noticed her mum was fast asleep and snoring.

Aw, bless! She was all puckered out! Ha, but you snooze, you lose. So upon getting downstairs and seeing her mother was fast asleep, she took one of her straight cigarettes out of the box, stuck it in her mouth and lit it.

'If you counted up all of your mum's cigarettes you'd nicked, I wonder how much money you'd owe her...' her father said.

'None because I'm your spawn,' Kat stated, lit it, on her way back down to the sofa, she took a deep drag of the cigarette and blew it in her father's face.

He couldn't help but cough but he was able to splutter one word out, 'why?'

'Oh, sorry my bad, I thought you wanted some.' She couldn't help but laugh as she said that and sat down.

'It may be early, but I could go for dinner, what about you?'

'I'm obviously down for whatever keeps me away from homework for longer, but warning I can't really be asked to cook.'

'Neither, so takeaway?'

'I could happily eat a pizza.' Kat, as if to really prove her point, got a pizza menu out and threw it at her dad.

'Does that mean I'm calling them to order?'

'If that's you offering, then yes.'

'OK and what am I ordering?'

'Well, I'll have sweet and sour chicken.'

'Shame then that Pizza Hut doesn't do Chinese...'

'Just get the regular?'

'OK, will do.' He then called them and ordered. 'Should be about half an hour,' he said when he hung up the phone.

It was then that her mother, rather violently, decided to wake up. She borderline shouted, 'Don't touch my croissants!' I think the shouting was what woke her up, to be honest. I wonder what she was dreaming about and what bastard would take her croissants? Good thing she had pizza on the way…

'Good morning, sleep well?' the father said.

The mother was still coming to, so she didn't reply.

'Pizza. En route,' the daughter said.

'Pizza? For breakfast?' Bless her! The mother was still out of it.

'Look outside. It's dark. It's not breakfast, he was joking.' Kat happily became the informant, so happily, in fact, that she laughed.

They all watched TV until the food arrived, Kat was so grateful for the ring of the doorbell, she was ready to eat. She even went up to the front door to collect it, she used her dad's contactless bank card to pay for it, shut the door and the food was all hers. So she went downstairs to eat it with her parents, the food did make her feel better, she munched away greedily. Then they all had a post-meal cigarette, Kat actually rolled this time, then she looked at the clock and sighed.

'I unfortunately still have homework, so I got to go upstairs and do it but thank you for the pizza, I'll probably watch something upstairs after, so see you tomorrow?'

'Yes, of course, darling, see you tomorrow,' the father said. The mother said nothing, she just waved.

So Kat went back upstairs and returned to her room, where the joys of homework took place. Being there reminded her to check her phone because downstairs she was too busy with food. But wait, but shouldn't being upstairs remind her to work hard? Yes, but after playing hard…

Ages ago, Dominic had replied to her text, it said, *as a friend or as a bell end? Check out my rhyming.*

Kat chuckled and said, *actually maybe therapy will be good for you…*

He then replied rather quickly, *Har de fucking har, I'm glad that questionable sense of humour is still there.*

What sense of humour? I was being serious?

Never change. Was all he said. She just smiled and put her phone down, it was time for the more mentally stimulating task of homework. She had to look over and revise her notes from Chemistry for later in the week, so she wasn't that bothered by revising it all now, she would let her short-term memory come into play, just before the test began. She maybe spent ten minutes looking through her notes, she did have other homework, but was she going to do it? I'll let you guess…

When her Chemistry was as good as done, well, she had briefly read through her notes, she quickly decided on a film to watch, the last Lord of the Rings was a perfect idea. So she put the DVD on and watched the film. It was quite a long film, well, they all are long, but it was long enough to warrant going to bed after, so that's what she did, but after her daily dose of self-harm and brushing her teeth.

Wasn't she good for brushing her teeth? Even she didn't want cavities. But after brushing, it was time for cutting, I guess another version of BC? Brushing and cutting? Seeing the blood was strangely relaxing, it was needed, she thought it was what she deserved. After cutting herself, she put her phone on charge, set her alarm on it for the next day and properly settled herself into bed and went to sleep, it didn't take her too long to fall asleep. Her fucked up routine had its uses, it helped her fall asleep.

Chapter 7

When her alarm went off the next day, her response was groaning. School! Gross! She followed the same routine for getting up as she did on Friday, well, she dressed herself. Well, her Monday at school, was very much the same as her Friday without the whole talking Dominic out of suicide business. It was a much calmer and nicer situation when she saw Dominic, they even had lunch together, so they had become quite good friends, he even accompanied her for a cigarette on the roof of the Science Block.

'God, it feels weird to be back here.' He even let a tear shed.

'Oh shit, forget about my cigarette, we can go if you want?'

'No, no, it's cool, don't worry, I just need to focus on the positive things about this place, for example meeting you.'

'Have you ever been told you're so sweet?'

He laughed. 'Well, you know what, I'm aware I'm so sweet, I even thought it was a good trait to put on my CV...'

Well, that set off Kat's laughter. 'I know we've spoken about my humour, but my God, check out the big brains on Dominic...'

Dominic then started bowing, 'Why thank you.'

The rest of the day was bog-standard and fairly boring, well, the rest of the week was fairly boring, nothing really happened, apart from Kat and Dominic got closer.

Kat sailed into the weekend, well, her Friday night, it was going to be a bog-standard weekend for her, as far as she knew anyway, at home. You know typical. She ate dinner with her parents that night, again normal.

Then, after eating and cleaning up the Kitchen table of all the dirty plates and stuff, they all smoked a cigarette in the Living Room in front of the TV. When he was finished, the father quickly went upstairs and came back downstairs, but Kat took no notice, she thought he was only going to the toilet, but no, that's not what he did at all…

'Do you want to do anything tonight?' the father asked his family upon sitting back down in his chair.

'Do anything? Like what?' was Kat's response.

'Yeah, like play a game?'

'Is that you saying you want a beating at Poker?'

'Yes, I would love to win at Poker.' That was that. He went to go sit at the Kitchen table, while Kat got the Poker out, then sat down and her mother went to join them. When they were all sat there, but before they started playing, the father whipped out the little mirror he had used previously with his friend and had now acquired a little straw rather than a banknote, he was moving up in the world…

Ha, literally, by getting high. He then and this is where it gets really quite fucked, but he pulled out a little baggie filled with white powder, Kat was unable to say anything, so she just stared. He poured some of the white powder onto the mirror and pulled a razor out that was in his pocket, to cut it up. You know, just a casual family Friday night…

Again Kat just stared, I think she had gone into shock, he was acting like this was the most normal thing, but weren't parents supposed to stop their children from doing drugs? Not actually take them with their kids? I understand parents wanting to be their child's friend, but wasn't this taking it a little too far? OK, not a little, but a ridiculously big amount of too far, like seven marathon amounts of too far…?

The father had made three lines, one for each of them, how sweet! Sharing is caring! It was his turn first, so he snorted the line-up and breathed out, then he passed and put the mirror in front of Kat. Again she stared, it wasn't like she hadn't taken cocaine before, but with her parents? That was a whole other ball park, no forget ball park, this was a whole other game…A game she didn't know how to play…

Before taking anything she said 'I think I need a drink, one sec.' So she went to get a drink, so fucking what if she was underage? Her parents weren't allowed to give a flying fuck now, oh sorry Mr Officer, is underage drinking illegal? I don't know about you but I think snorting cocaine is more illegal. So she got herself a gin, took a deep swig and sat back down. Her father was maybe halfway through a bottle of wine, so he wasn't exactly drunk and her mother was stone-cold sober, so had she entered The Twilight Zone or something?

When she sat down, she kept hold of her gin and again just stared at the mirror that was now in front of her.

'Don't feel you have to.' Aw! How fatherly! Except, no not really…

'No, I'll do it, I've done it before but jeez,' she then made a joke, 'does this mean you want to lose at Poker for an extra-long amount of time?' She said because cocaine didn't exactly put you to sleep, it kept you awake.

'OK then, do that, then deal.'

She had her orders from her father, do that. Do that? Well, it was just a cheeky line, so she did as she was told, she did it. She snorted the cheeky line.

It felt cleaner, well, better than what she had snorted before, probably because her parents actually had money and were able to buy better shit, a teenager's budget is fairly limited. But regardless, snorting it felt rather strange as well as good, so Kat took another deep swig of gin, her glass was now empty enough to warrant getting another drink, so she did just that. While her mother took her line to complete The Holy Trinity, how lovely!

Then, for about an hour normality resumed, playing Poker with chit-chat, but Kat knew it was far from normal. As far away from normal as you could possibly get, bizarre was a good word, what the actual fuck was a good phrase. Kat controlled the music, she was the resident DJ, she just played regular happy shit…

The father then decided it was time. Time to do what? The Hokey-Pokey? Close, but no, another line, which was as bizarre as several Hokey-Pokeys. So, the father brought out the baggie only because everything else was still on the table from earlier, it was strange how this was only the second line, but it already felt normal. Kat's gin glass was empty. But she no longer felt the need to have it full to take the line. Sharing really is caring…

This repeated a few times until the parents thought it was late enough in the a.m. to warrant going to bed and trying to sleep, but Kat was still far too awake for that shit, cocaine can do that, it keeps you awake. So, her parents stood up, she walked a few steps to the adjoining Living Room and stuck the TV on.

'Good night!' Kat shouted to her parents as they walked towards the stairs.

'Night!' her father shouted back and they left and went upstairs. That was that.

Complete.

Finished.

They were both acting so normal? Maybe she was being the strange one? Maybe that was a perfectly normal situation to be in? Maybe it was normal and she was just being strange? They certainly acted like it was normal...

So she got her phone out knowing full well that anyone who was even vaguely normal would be asleep, but she decided to send a text, no it wasn't to Ben and it wasn't to Juliet. You know the people closest to her...It was to Dominic. Lucky sod...

*When we're both awake, can I call? I need you; well, I need a friend...*was what she said. She pressed send.

The message was sent, she now needed to cut, she needed pain, she needed something, so she went upstairs to brush her teeth and go to her room. When she was brushing her teeth, was when she looked into the bathroom mirror and she just cried, it was all she could do. When her teeth were finished, but her crying was not, she decided to go up to her room, when she got there she grabbed her knife, she didn't even sit down and just had it on her wrist while standing up.

Perhaps her blood was flowing more freely tonight or she had just had at it with more force than usual, but there was definitely more blood. Quite frankly, she was desperate, the whole evening was an awful lot to take in, no it was just ridiculous, there was taking something, there was taking something in, then there was this. Whatever this was. The sun was even starting to rise now, that's how late it was, it was now early.

In sheer desperation she actually considered calling Dominic, it was daytime? Kind of? OK not really…Upon thinking about it a little she decided not to call him, it was definitely the wrong time, she would talk to him tomorrow, all would be revealed tomorrow. So that was when she decided to get in bed, she turned her bedroom light off, put her phone on charge, got in bed, covered all of herself with the duvet, even her head, so she couldn't see the light coming from outside, there was a vague method in her madness and then she went to sleep.

Her phone, as per, was put on silent while she slept…

She fell asleep fairly quickly, it was a good, restful and uninterrupted sleep, surprisingly. When she awoke it was still daylight, so she hadn't slept through the whole day like she was expecting to, but she would've happily slept for longer, well forever…She then reached for her phone and checked it; aw, Ben was missing her! How sweet! So, she replied fairly quickly, that was easy. The rest of her phone not so much…

She had a whopping fifteen missed calls and twenty texts from, you guessed it, Dominic. To summarise his texts, he basically said:

Yes, of course, you can call and next time you can call me any time of the day or night, I'm here for you. You were there for me, so let me be there for you, I'm an atheist but I fucking pray you're not replying because you're sleeping and not…

In a matter of minutes after reading it, she replied with, *You're atheist? Me too, kind of thought you were a member of the God squad there...But sorry, was asleep. Late night.*

In seconds, almost as if he was staring at his phone, waiting for Kat to reply he called her, she answered.

'Hi, how can I help you?' Kat said.

'Oh, thank Christ...' He deeply exhaled. 'Yeah, can I get a number fifteen and a number fifty with ketchup please?'

Kat laughed. 'Sorry, sir, we've run out of number fifteen...'

'I'm just going to say this, you really worried me there, knowing your past...' Dominic said, OK time for them to have a serious talk now, Kat may have wished she was, but she was no longer a takeaway...

'Sorry, I was asleep.'

'I know, I was just worried it could be forever. No, wrong word I wasn't worried, you get worried if you're fucking takeaway is on the way, I was fucking terrified.' Kat could hear Dominic starting to cry as he said that.

'Don't worry, that thought didn't even cross my mind, cutting was enough.'

'Again I say thank Christ. What even happened?'

'Nothing, I just got drunk.'

'Jeez? Really? I would've thought if you really were drunk you would've been unable to text and you would've passed out well before you sent it, so credit to you.'

'Does that mean you believe me?'

'Not in the slightest...'

'Fuck.'

'No, calm down, there's no need to swear and use profanity, just talk to me, but remember make it suitable for a younger audience,' he laughed, 'like me.'

'I'm sorry, I can't, I just can't, not like this, not on the phone.'

'Is that you saying you want to meet up?'

'No, that's me saying let's set up a lunch meeting for next week.'

Dominic started laughing. 'You know you can say lunch date, right? I'm not a client and I know you're taken.'

Kat joined in with the laughter. 'Not a client? Do you want a number fifty or not?'

'Wow, you actually made a good joke, consider me impressed.'

'Unnecessary. Right, I'm going to go and get me some breakfast.'

'Breakfast? But it's mid-afternoon?'

'So? It's still my breakfast?'

'You, do you.'

'I always do.'

Kat saw that as a good time to end the call, so she did and went downstairs to get some food, her parents were awake and watching TV.

'Good day, notice how I'm not saying good morning…' her father said through laughter. But Kat didn't reply, she was too focused on her goal, food.

Who gives a shit at what time it was? It was just a late breakfast? She still made herself a big bowl of cereal and practically inhaled it and afterwards she inhaled something. Ooh was it nitrous oxide? No. Was it cocaine? No, don't be ridiculous, it was a Sunday. It was only a cigarette. Nice try.

At the same time, her father stuck some show on, that they all watched, on the TV. They watched quite a few episodes, well, they had been recorded, so they could watch them anytime. Notice how nothing has been mentioned about last night, a new normal? Or just a fucked-up situation? Who fucking knows?

When it was early evening and they had just finished another episode, the father didn't put on another episode, he instead asked a one worded question, 'dinner?'

'Yes, I took something out of freezer and left it on the side to defrost,' the mother said and she got up from her chair and went to go check on it, checking on it entailed poking and prodding it to make sure it had thawed. It had. So she put the oven on and filled a baking tray with the freshly thawed food and some chips from the freezer. While she was waiting for the oven to be hot enough to put the food in, she did some washing up, perfect timing! When the washing up was done, the oven was ready, so she put the food in and went to go sit down in her chair.

From then on, their Saturday night was very similar to their Friday night, it was very PC, like what I did there? PC? No, not personal computer. Poker and cocaine. It also finished very similarly to her Friday night because her parents went up to bed before her. So she watched TV, cut her wrist and texted Dominic, in that order. There wasn't much to watch on TV, especially given the time and she hadn't recorded anything, so she went up to her room to cut and to go to bed.

Then it was self-harm time. Her favourite time of the day! No, not really...Tonight she actually sat down on her bed to do it, did it make her feel better? I don't even know what it made her feel anymore...Pain? Well, obviously not or she wouldn't do it. Oh dear, just say it, I'm a shit narrator, hey Kat, when you're done with that knife, pass it here. I don't think she heard me…Bugger.

She then messaged Dominic, her text to him said *actually can I reschedule our meeting to Sunday, rather than Monday?* This time, she sent it just before getting into bed, I think it was earlier than yesterday, well, the sun wasn't up, it was still dark outside. She put her phone on charge, made sure it was on silent and got into bed, it took her longer to fall asleep, what with all the cocaine floating around her system but she fell asleep, eventually.

Chapter 8

When she awoke, she was ready, oh no wait, no she wasn't. Ready for what? Tears? Wasn't her life fucked up enough? She felt she had to steady herself for the day ahead, she steadied herself by getting her breathing in check because when she awoke it was all over the place. Maybe she was mid-nightmare and that's why she woke up? She was borderline panting, so it could be possible...She then checked her phone, her breathing now felt normal, well, as normal as it was going to get.

She received a text from Dominic, no, not just a text, but an essay. He said, of course, *you can reschedule the meeting for whenever you want, today is fine, I'm just here for the ride, but just be aware if you're going to send me a text like that, you can at least give me your address. Because I would've come over before you woke up, I wouldn't have even woken you up, I would've let you wake up naturally.*

Look, things are hard for us anyway, aha I think mental is the right word to describe us, but if you've now got some big other thing, I want to help, so let me help. I'm not even going to try calling you, my calls did nothing yesterday, you're just a bastard who puts their phone on silent, aren't you?

She laughed at the last part, other than the laughter all she did was text him her address, he replied momentarily with a *cheers.*

I can't believe how easy that was and how little was said, it was done and dusted, he could be her next-door neighbour or live on the other side of the world. She just didn't know, so she had no idea how long it would take him to get there.

She assumed he was coming over, even though it wasn't explicitly said, but why else would he want her address? So, she decided it was time to get dressed. She didn't even decide she didn't give a fuck about how she looked because she just didn't give a fuck, so she settled on a tracksuit, comfort was key. She was now ready to socialise, well, she was dressed and quite frankly, that would have to be good enough…

She then went downstairs, it was earlier than yesterday, but still afternoon, just like yesterday her parents were up and watching TV.

'Just so you know, my friend is coming over and we'll go out and probably get some food.' Kat thought it was best to tell them…

'OK, no worries,' the mother said. 'When?'

'He's en route, I think.'

'He? A boy? Is Ben not enough for you?' the father decided to join the conversation with an awful joke.

'What century are you living in? I have plenty of friends who are guys?'

He answered with a, 'No need to get touchy, I was only asking…'

'Well, maybe next time, don't ask.'

She was sat on the sofa, then decided to roll herself a cigarette and smoked it, the father played something on the

TV, that they all watched, but Kat didn't really watch it, she was too busy thinking about how she would lie to Dominic. She couldn't be honest, she just couldn't. The best lie she came up with was saying she was fine but it was just time of the month weirdness, so complete and utter shit? Yes, something like that...After about half an hour of sitting there, she received a text.

It was from Dominic, he said *OK, not going to ring the doorbell because I don't know what's going off, but I think I'm here. So, can you come get me...Please...Help...*

She replied straight away with an *OK, coming.*

'I think muggins is here, going to go. He texted.'

'OK, have fun!' the mother said.

'Will do!' So, Kat went upstairs to put some shoes and a coat on, she made sure she had all the basics, such as phone, keys and money, etcetera, etcetera, etcetera. When she was ready, she opened the front door and smiled because she expected to see her guest...

That was weird, she couldn't see him anywhere. Had he gotten lost? She was about to text him. But then she saw his reflection hiding behind her car in another car.

'Oh, woe is me, he must've gotten lost.' She put a hand on her head as if she was in complete and utter dismay.

'You fucker. Woe is me? Did you see me?' Dominic said as he let his presence be known and he stood up.

'Obviously. In a reflection, who fucking says woe is me, seriously?' She shut her door behind her and skipped down to meet him, she hugged him.

'Where to?' he asked.

'Late lunch?'

'Not going to lie, I was kind of hoping you'd want to eat, I have hunger, so, yes, let's go eat something please.'

There was a whole village of restaurants minutes away, so they walked off her road to check them out, they quickly settled on pizza, so they went to the pizza joint. The lady who sat them down was very welcoming, she gave them each a menu, took their drinks orders of one coke and one diet coke and left. When she came back with the drinks, they were ready to order food, blimey, weren't they easy customers? So, they ordered their food, she took their menus and that was that, so she left.

Now, it was time for waiting, which meant conversation, bugger…

'OK, so talk to me?' Dominic said softly.

'Qué?'

'Talk to me.'

'Huh, lo siento solo hablo español.' Translation: Sorry, I only speak Spanish.

'Bien, si quieres jugar el juego de habla español puedo jugar eso.' Translation: Fine, if you want to play the Spanish speaking game, I can play that.

'Bastardo…' If you need that translating, I'm sorry, you're thick.

'I know, I know, what can I say? I'm just a Spanish-speaking, surprise,' Dominic laughed as he said it.

Kat grumbled and took a swig of her drink.

'Given you haven't started speaking yet about anything serious, I'm going to assume it's not an easy topic of conversation, but I hope you know you can talk to me, about anything.' He reached for her hand and held it.

She started laughing. 'No, don't worry, I'm OK, really, I've just been acting weird because of my period.' Nailed it?

He then went and stood up. 'OK then, when you're ready to talk to me, seriously, I'm right here, text me.'

He took a few steps towards the exit when Kat said, 'No, it's cool, I'm ready, come back here, I'm sorry, should've known period shit wouldn't work with you…'

He came back to the table. 'Thank God, you're ready, I'm starving.'

'Starving maybe. Funny, not so much.'

'Like you're one to talk about humour?' he said, but then he started laughing.

'Well, given by profession I'm a clown, I'd say yes, I am one to talk about humour…'

'Serious talk time?'

'In an ideal world I'd answer no, never, but not if you'll leave…'

'Well, I will, so I'm all ears.' He leaned back in his chair as if he was getting ready to hear her tell a bountiful story.

'Fuck. OK. So, I've had quite the bizarre weekend…' She lowered her voice, just in case anyone could hear and was listening. 'To start, the reason I was up so late was because of this little white powder…'

'Not going to lie I kind of assumed it was because of drugs… You seemed so unhappy…' Kat then started crying.

'No, shh, don't cry, I'm right here.'

'But I am unhappy? And who did I?' She blew her nose into her napkin. 'Who did I do them with? Whose were they?'

'How am I supposed to know? A friend?'

'You're so cold.'

'Um, your cousin, three times removed?'

'Warmer, but no.'

'I give up.'

'Starts with P.'

'Fuck, pets can be crafty buggers, can't they?'

'Not pet.'

'I kind of gathered…'

Then a silence ensued for a while, Dominic didn't know what to say, but luckily the waitress brought their pizzas over in the silence…

Out of courtesy Dominic thanked her, but Kat didn't thank her, her hunger was gone anyway, in fact she wished she was gone.

'I'm so sorry, I just don't know what to say, that's some quite serious shit,' he said and started cutting his pizza into slices, but Kat didn't, she just stared at the floor instead. 'Please eat,' Dominic asked.

'Hunger has died; hey, maybe I should die.'

Dominic slammed his knife down, on the table, hard, his food was no longer important. 'Don't you fucking dare give me, of all people, that shit.'

Very little, OK no eating happened during their meal, no talking either, very strange…Kat's eyes remained on the floor whereas Dominic's eyes remained on Kat. Then the waitress came over and took their plates.

'Aw, are you just not hungry today?' she said.

'Something like that,' was Dominic's answer.

'Should I wrap these up for you?' she asked.

'Can't say I'm bothered, what about you, Kat?' She just shook her head in answer. 'I think we're good thanks, can we just get the bill please?'

'Coming right up,' and just like that, she was gone with their full plates.

'At this point, I'll even accept a conversation about the weather, you're scaring me with your silence.' Dominic finally decided to speak to Kat! Result!

'Yeah, well, my parents scared me with their snorting,' Kat borderline whispered, just as the waitress dropped off their bill.

'Fuck, of course, I'm sorry.'

'Don't be, life is just a piss take.'

'You can say that again…'

'OK, so what's the damage? Split it two ways?'

'No, you can jog on.'

'But I don't jog? No, but seriously, accept my money!'

'How about I'll take that thought into consideration.' But he didn't take that thought into consideration, he lied.

Then the waitress appeared with a card machine and Dominic paid for it all, in its entirety. Dominic said, 'Thank you,' to the waitress and she left.

But instead of saying thank you to Dominic, you know, like a normal person would do, Kat just said, 'You bastard.' Aw, how sweet!

'Where to now?' Dominic, the bastard, asked.

'Well, if you want, I could walk you to the train station or there's a big field we could go sit on and talk?'

'Well, I'm not ready to leave yet and I don't think you're ready for me to leave yet, am I right or am I right?'

'So field?'

'Yes.'

'Field is one word and one word alone, hey, here's a thought, maybe you should try using it next time…'

'OK, fine, but go on.' He started poking her. 'Answer my question.'

'Are you right?' Kat started laughing. 'No, you're Dominic.'

'You're a cruel clown.'

'Clown school was hard on me, what can I say?'

The field was only minutes away, so they walked to the field and arrived there fairly quickly, well, they arrived there in minutes. They sat down opposite each other.

'Kind of starting to regret not taking away my pizza...'

'OK, fine, cool, OK, will sir let me buy him a snack?'

'If I'm a sir then surely I have enough money to buy myself a snack?' Kat started to scowl. 'OK, yes, fine, you can buy me a snack, please don't hurt me.' He leaned back so far that he was now lying down on the grass.

'What do you even want?'

'Does that mean I'm not allowed to come? If not, then surprise me.'

'So, one large batch of surprise me? On it.' Kat stood up and walked towards the shops, she got the usual, a meal deal, a bag of crisps, a sandwich and a bar of chocolate, then she had an idea, a dastardly idea. She made sure everything else would fit in her pockets first, they did, so she grabbed a jar of baby food, when she had paid for everything, she put all normal foods in her pockets and carried the baby food in her hand.

Then she walked towards the exit and spoke to herself and laughed 'watch him never say surprise me to me again.'

She held the baby food behind her back and walked back towards the field where he was sitting, whilst now, trying to hold in her laughter.

'Excellent service! That was quick, what did you get me?'

'Close your eyes and hold out your hand.'

'Bit kinky, but OK.' So, he did as was instructed of him.

She put the baby food in his hand, she couldn't hold in her laughter anymore.

'The suspense is killing me; can I open my eyes yet? It feels like a jar...'

She was laughing even more now, she couldn't even get the word yes out so she just said, 'Mmhmm.'

So, that was when he opened his eyes, upon looking at his hand he said, 'No, no, no, you've got it all wrong, I'm fourteen years old, not fourteen months old.'

'Oops,' she said and started rolling herself a cigarette.

'As long as you're alright with your smokes.'

Before lighting it, she took out the rest of her edible shopping. He grabbed the sandwich and in seconds he had shoved it into his gob.

'You're welcome,' Kat said and lit her cigarette.

The food was necessary, he needed it, in between a mouthful of food, he raised his hand and said, 'So please continue.'

'There's nothing more to say, I guess my parents are as fucked up as me, just in a different way, no, not even in a different way because I do drugs too.'

'But you're not a parent? Look, I understand the whole "be friends with your kids" thing, but isn't that taking it too far?'

'It is what it is, I guess.'

'It's your life, so your decision, but is there anything you want to do? It's your choice obviously, but just know I'm with you no matter what you decide.'

'Do anything? Like what? A cheeky line?'

'I love how even in a what the fuck situation, you can still make a joke,' he started laughing, 'if you can even call that a joke…'

Her answer was violence, in the form of hitting him.

'Last, I'll say on the matter, but just know I'm here for you.'

'Here? But it's so much nicer over there?'

His laughter continued, 'OK, fine, I don't know where I am, I could be anywhere, but I'm here for you.'

'Much better.'

They carried on with chit-chat for a while, until Dominic decided it was time he should probably go home, so Kat took him to the train station. Before going in, Kat gave him a hug as if to thank him for everything.

The last thing he said to her was, 'I'm here for you.' Well, that only resulted in her giving him another hug.

When the hugging was over, he went down the stairs to the platform and left. She didn't want him to go and for normality to resume, but that's what him leaving meant, so she walked home. Socialising was done for the day. When she got home, she went downstairs for a cigarette and many, many questions, just your bog standard 'how was it?' And 'did you have a nice time?' And questions of that nature.

The questions all happened in the space of time it took to roll and smoke a cigarette. When her cigarette was finished, she decided to go up to her room. She had homework, but was she going to do it? Absolutely not. Instead, she just relaxed on her laptop, she could just lie and say she forgot instead of saying, sorry miss I didn't do it because I was too busy thinking about cocaine.

I'm not sure how well that would go down…

Chapter 9

She just relaxed on her laptop for hours, until she saw it as late enough to get ready for bed, so that's what she did. She put her laptop away, went downstairs to one of her many bathrooms, oh yeah, her house was big, if her parents could afford cocaine, they could afford a big house...But she brushed her teeth and I really shouldn't have to tell you the last thing on her bedtime routine, hint it involves a knife. Yes! That's right! Cutting bread! She wanted toast tomorrow for breakfast, what can I say?

After cutting herself...

Wait what happened to the bread?

AFTER CUTTING HERSELF, it was time to get in bed, so she did just that, it wasn't ridiculously late, just a nice time for the end of the day. She put her phone on charge, the alarm on and fell asleep fairly fast, not ridiculously fast, in an adequate amount of time, she fell asleep, as per, holding onto her wrist.

When it was the next morning, her alarm woke her up, so she turned it off, with disdain, she didn't want to be up, sleeping was so much more fun, hence why she wanted to do it forever. She then stood up and got dressed, the disdain was still there, when there were clothes on her body she went downstairs. It was breakfast time. She had cereal even though she prepared so much bread the night before, oh no wait, no she didn't...

As per, she arrived at school via coach and also as per, she stayed plugged into her iPod, it was safer that way and no socialising whatsoever, which was a bonus, OK, it was the main reason she did it. She only unplugged herself when she arrived for period one, which was maths. Oh, joy! Then period two, which was Biology. She then received a text ten minutes before Biology finished, which was ten minutes before the start of break.

It said *top of the morning to you! Would you care to meet me for a smoke during break?* Dominic asked.

Ugh, if I must was her reply.

When her Biology lesson was over and it was break, she went up the stairs to the roof and started rolling. As soon as she was done, within seconds Juliet appeared, wait, I thought she was meeting Dominic? Ah, yes, but where else could she go to school and smoke?

Juliet asked, 'Howdy, how was your weekend?'

'A mess,' was Kat's reply.

Juliet was going to ask how, but that was when Dominic appeared, so his appearance saved Kat from having that conversation, for now...

'Are you guys going out or something now? I swear you're always together...' Juliet jokingly asked, she knew the answer...

Dominic laughed, hard. 'No, I'm just playing the long game.'

Juliet joined in with the laughter. 'Good luck!'

'Shall I just go?' Kat said, she wasn't laughing, no, not at all.

'Lighten up!' Juliet said and hit Kat on the shoulder, then her laughter increased, 'or I'll do it, I'll jump!'

Dominic laughed at that, but Kat didn't, she stood up, finished her cigarette and left. 'See you at lunch, I guess,' was her finishing statement because she then left them to it.

The middle part of her school day was bog-standard and boring, but oh joy, she got a litter duty for not doing her History homework. Well, she saw herself as litter, so she deserved to pick it up, surely? Then lunch came around slowly but surely. She decided on a sandwich and sat down, on her own, she wasn't feeling particularly social, so she plugged herself back into her iPod, it was safer that way, but then Dominic sat down opposite her with his hot food. So much for not being social? So she unplugged herself from her headphones and just stared at him.

For the longest time, no words were uttered, until Dominic said, 'to quote Pulp Fiction,' he coughed as if to clear his throat, 'that's when you know you've found somebody really special. When you can just shut the fuck up for a minute and comfortably share silence.'

'Isn't Pulp Fiction out of your age range?' She laughed.

But he got his comeback out quickly and steadily, 'And isn't smoking out of yours?'

'Touché. Speaking of which, eat up! I want one.'

So he finished his food, put his tray away with all the other dirty ones and they went up to the roof of the Science Block, Kat hoped and prayed Juliet didn't come, she messed up the karma between Kat and Dominic. Kat quickly rolled.

'So how are you anyway, be honest with me?' he asked her just as she was about to spark her cigarette.

'All over the shop is my honest response, fine is my not-so-honest response. You can choose which one you heard…' She sparked her cigarette.

'Have you had to spend the day being not so honest?'

'Not being honest is why I'm here, at school, but I just couldn't stay at home, that would've been worse.'

'No, that's fine, I understand.' He put his arms around her, 'I'm here for you, whatever you need, know that.'

'I really appreciate that.'

'You're welcome.' Then he started laughing and said, 'Your bloody folks are bloody daft, don't make me bloody laugh, oh bloody hell I think we're evidently in chicken town…'

'Wow. Consider me impressed…Good reference…You know John Cooper Clarke…How punk rock…'

'Just because I eat baby food, does not mean I was born yesterday,' he said in reference to what she bought him yesterday.

She started laughing. 'You crack me up.'

'That's because you're an egg.'

Her laughter continued, 'an egg?'

'Of the scrambled variety…'

'Well, at least I like myself, wait, no, that's bad, isn't it?'

'Eating yourself is certainly an interesting way to go…Bit strange though, I would've just gone for jumping off a building, but that's just me…'

'OK, we've exhausted the topic of my sense of humour, why don't we talk about yours?'

'We shouldn't talk about it because that was a serious statement.'

Kat just started laughing. 'You just do you.'

The beginning of their relationship may have been unconventional, but I think it's safe to say they now needed each other. They had similar problems and similar senses of humour; they were just similar in many if not all aspects. No shit he fancied her, but she couldn't fancy him even if she wanted to, she was taken.

Her cigarette was finished and so was lunchtime, so they went downstairs, left the Science Block and joined their forms. The rest of the day was bog-standard and boring, in fact the rest of the week was, until Friday lunchtime, Dominic and Kat now regularly ate lunch together, so they were sat opposite each other.

'It's Friday, how are you feeling about tonight? And, well, about um parents?'

'I'm feeling that whatever will be, will be.'

'Just know you can text me whenever, I may be asleep, but text me, yeah? Promise?'

'Am I even allowed to say no?'

'You can say what you want, as long as it starts in y and ends in s.'

'OK, fine.' She thought for minute, 'Yetis? There's even an e in it, I'm guessing you were going to make that an extra qualification.'

'So I say text me and you say yetis? Are you, you know, OK up there?' He pointed to and held his head.

She started laughing, which only made him start laughing too. Then he accompanied her for a cigarette, they had two more periods and then they were done with school for the week, bring on the weekend! A nice relaxing weekend, that's what Kat needed, shame, that's not what she was going to get.

Kat went and sat on her coach, with her headphones on and music blaring. Then she received a text, from, you guessed it, Dominic, it said *yetis? Or years?* That made her laugh, well, it made her chuckle.

I must say I prefer yetis; years are so long... was her reply.

He replied quick enough *text me, yeah? Let me know what's occurring.*

What's occurring? I'm sorry have we entered Little Britain?

Careful, I think you're showing your age there, Little what? he said.

So, she said *oh fuck off.*

The coach then reached her stop and it was time to get off. Her house was only minutes away, so it didn't take her long at all to walk there, when she got there she dumped off all her school stuff, like her bag and her shoes and went downstairs for a cigarette, her parents were still working, probably to pay for the coke habit, so the TV was off.

So, she sat at the Kitchen table and rolled herself a cigarette.

'Dinner soon?' the father asked.

'Yeah, sure, what do you want?' she said in between drags.

'I think your mother has defrosted something.'

But the mother didn't say anything, she was too engrossed in whatever work she was doing on her computer.

'Does that mean I'm cooking?' Kat asked.

'I think so...' the father said.

So Kat got on with cooking, even though it was so early, but at least it was fairly easy, just putting things in the oven, cooking and preparing vegetables was not important, her dad didn't touch them anyway unless you count potatoes. When the food was all ready, they all ate at the Kitchen table and afterwards went to go sit down and watch TV in the Living Room and have a cigarette. How normal!

When the father was finished, he went upstairs to put a jumper on, oh no wait, no he didn't, although what he did do did make him warmer...When he came back downstairs he told Kat to go to his room, Kat wasn't thick, she could guess why, so she went up there, more because she felt she had to than actually wanting to.

She snorted the line that had been made and left out for her up in his room and went back downstairs.

The first thing her father said when she was back in the Living Room, but before she had even sat down was 'game?'

'I feel like I've lived this before, is it last weekend?' was her response.

'Oh, I'm sorry, I just want to spend time with my family, is that not OK?' You forgot to mention you also want to snort large quantities of blow...

Kat didn't even answer, she just grabbed the Poker and went to go sit at the Kitchen table, it didn't take long for her family to join her, but before sitting down, the mother went upstairs to her room to do a cheeky line. So this, whatever this was, was now normal? Um OK then...

After hours and many lines later, the father decided it was time for him to go to bed. How responsible! It was getting quite late! Ha responsible my ass…But Kat wasn't quite ready for bed yet so she went and watched TV, well, she put it on and stared at her phone, she wanted to text Dominic, but couldn't, she thought it was best not to. She went upstairs, did her usual routine and went to sleep. That was her Friday fun day over!

When she awoke, the first thing she did was check her phone, it was early afternoon, Dominic had texted her.

I'm going to take you not texting as a positive?

The question mark was like him asking, is it a positive? But she didn't reply, she just left her phone in her room and went downstairs. Her Saturday was very similar, if not the same as her last Saturday, it was very white and snowy…A new routine had come about.

She didn't even check her phone when she came back upstairs to bed, it was a Sunday chore. So she cut herself and went to sleep, like usual, she just needed to feel something. Anything. Even pain. No, especially pain.

When she awoke on the Sunday, the first thing she did was check her phone, it was early afternoon, so not too late, then she checked her texts, she had one from Ben that was just continuing their ongoing, constant conversation. Nice to know she didn't reply for a day and he didn't give a shit.

Whereas it was quite clear Dominic did give a shit, he had texted, oh boy had he texted. I'm not going to type each message out, fuck that shit, I'm going to put my summarisation skills to good use...If you can even call them skills...

But he basically said in many short messages...*Don't just blank me, I care. Talk to me, in Spanish if you really want but preferably in English...How has your weekend been? Restful? Normal? Or just like last weekend?*

That's my main question...I should've really asked it first, it's kind of important...Take that as my starting point. Well, I shouldn't have to ask it anyway, but here we are...But don't forget about my other messages. Please say something, anything. To say I'm worried is putting it lightly. Don't make me come over there to check you're not dead because watch this space, I will. Your fault that I now know your address.

Sorry! Was asleep, I'm fine was Kat's reply.

For a whole day? I thought I could sleep, but jeez. He was very good at replying straight away, it only took him a few minutes.

Sorry!

So, talk to me? Dominic asked and requested but Kat took that as her cue to go downstairs for a casual hit of nicotine, texting was for losers anyway. So she left her phone in her room, left her room and went downstairs.

It was just another normal cocaine-free Sunday, it's not like her parents were bonkers with their cocaine usage, who do you take them for? Oh wait, no that's wrong...It was bonkers they had a usage in the first place...Whoops...

She fed herself and maybe stupidly asked her father, 'Why cocaine and why now?'

'I like it. It's fun. Don't you find it fun?'

Fucked is what I find it father. But Kat only thought those words, she didn't say them out loud, she just nodded.

But Kat did some homework later in her room, what a good little egg! Dominic had texted her again. But did Kat check? You can bet your bottom dollar that she didn't. What a good little chicken! Phones are too much of a distraction from the all-important homework anyway.

She has graduated from egg to chicken…She was done talking about the problem that was her life, no, she was just done in general. Living shouldn't be this hard. But it was. Time for normality! Phone on charge, alarm set and sleep! No, but first, cutting. The slices were harsh but necessary, it was good pain if that even exists…She needed it, well, she felt she needed it. She just stared at her blood as it left her body.

Chapter 10

Like usual, her alarm on her phone woke her up for the next day, so she turned it off, she wished she hadn't turned it on in the first place... Was she ready to face the day? Was she ready to face anything? I'm not even going to answer that...

But she just lay there, in bed, for a while and, maybe stupidly checked her texts, she saw that he once an hour, every hour, all night, yes all night, so he must've used an alarm to wake himself up and send it, but Dominic thought he needed to ask her hourly to talk to him. It's a little hard to talk to someone when you're asleep...

She laughed and replied with a s*orry, I don't talk to smelly people, pee yoo, I can smell you from here.*

He replied almost instantly with a *but I had a big shower three years ago, are you sure it's me you can smell?*

His response kept her laughter going, but she didn't send a reply, she just got ready for a day of learning. Learning! Her favourite thing to do! No, that's a shitty joke... When she was dressed, as per, she plugged herself into her iPod, went downstairs for breakfast and went to go catch her coach. She was happier today because she would get to go stay at her boyfriend's house this weekend. So one, an escape from her house and parents and two, she would get to see Ben and his parents knew they were sexually active so, at his, they were allowed to share a bed together. Get in!

Nothing really happened that day, until lunchtime, she was happily eating on her own, until Dominic, as per, sat down opposite her. God dammit. Socialising…But she just carried on eating and staring into space as if she hadn't seen him. She just wanted a peaceful quiet lunch, was that too much to ask for?

'I think you might know my question, you're not thick, so I'm not even going to ask it,' was the first thing he said to her.

'No, I only like cheese when it's melted on pizza,' was her response.

'I'm sorry, but what?'

'Wasn't your question about cheese?'

'Christ,' he then started eating and Kat continued with the staring, she let out a little chuckle too, at what she had said, but tried to hide it.

'I'm visiting my boyfriend this weekend, so I won't be at home which I think will make me happier, it'll be less fucked.'

'Does that mean it happened again?'

All she could think was *fuck, fuck, FUCK.*

But she said, 'Maybe,' in between a mouthful of food, deliberately, so it came out as complete and utter nonsense.

'Sorry, what? I don't speak gibberish.'

'Maybe,' she borderline shouted.

'Be aware, I'm taking that as a yes just so you know, but my God, that's so fucked, no offence to your parents.'

'No, be offensive, I don't give a shit.'

'But they did something right in making you?'

'How do you do that? How is it possible that you be sweet about me in a conversation that isn't even about me?'

'It's about the shit show that is your life though?' He started laughing. 'I didn't ask for these powers; they were thrust upon me.'

'Thrust? Aw, how sweet, did these powers give baby an orgasm?'

'Well, yes, actually...'

They both laughed, the rest of the week flew by, well, it didn't fly by, if it flew by, that insinuates they had fun, which they didn't, it slowly trudged by, until it got to Friday, Kat was so ready to get the train to Ben's house from school.

As per, she had lunch with Dominic on Friday.

'You deserve a nice peaceful weekend, so go have that with your boyfriend.'

'Planning on it.'

The rest of the day went by, not quick enough, but it went by, eventually, when it was finished, it was time for Kat to get the train up to see her boyfriend, the journey took around two hours, good thing Kat didn't care about the time, she saw the journey as worth it. When she arrived, her boyfriend met her on the platform and kissed her.

'How was your journey?' he asked her.

'Not so good, I died.'

'Oh shit, then I see dead people.'

'Nice to know I die and it's all about you.'

He kissed her again in response.

Then they left the station and embarked on the twenty-minute car journey to his house, his father drove.

When they arrived, the first thing Kat did was go upstairs and put her stuff in his room, well, their room, Ben followed her and almost as if to welcome her into his humble abode they slept together, then and there. When they were finished, they like usual watched a film, had dinner, watched another film and went to bed. Kat was just happy to be away from her home, not that it really felt like a home anymore, her house was just a house. But being at Ben's home meant no self-harm and no cocaine so that's something I guess…

She woke up fairly happily and fairly early for her Saturday, with the arms of her love around her, to really keep the romance going she woke him up with a wet willy. He groaned and grabbed his ear and shouted one word, 'Why?'

She rolled onto her back, 'Because,' she started laughing. 'You need to feed me.'

'Ugh, you're lucky I love you.'

'No, I'm not lucky, I'm hungry.'

Their Saturday consisted of watching stuff, food and the eating of which. Luckily Ben didn't have a rugby match that weekend, so he was just able to chill out. Sunday came too quickly, the day Kat had to leave, unfortunately.

It got to early afternoon, Kat would have to leave soon and go home, oh joy, so Ben wanted to have sex with her one more time before she left, typical teenager, so he started kissing her and she kissed him back. One thing led to another…They were ready, well, as ready as they would ever be. Then Ben moved her so she was facing away from him and he was on top, he was quite strong, well, he played rugby. It was a very raunchy position and very helpful for what was about to take place. Then he went inside her and started moving in and out. The movements were normal.

But wait. This wasn't normal. It hurt. It really fucking hurt. She started crying but she couldn't speak, she couldn't do or move anything, all she could do was focus on the pain. She wanted to scream, wrong hole! Because he was in her ass, but she couldn't, she couldn't do anything. She wanted normal sex, not this. He hadn't even spoken to her about doing this…I'm sorry, what? At least talk to her first…Wait, was this an r? I can't even say the full word. A rapture? No, still can't. Who knows how long it was before he came, but cum he did.

If you type rape definition into Google, this is what you get: unlawful sexual intercourse or any other sexual penetration of the vagina, anus or mouth of another person, with or without force, by a sex organ, other body part or foreign object, without the consent of the victim. The key word here is consent. She didn't give consent? He just took?

Silence encapsulated her for hours after, she just couldn't. Whereas Ben acted like that was the most normal thing.

This time it was the mother who drove Kat to the station, Ben was acting all normal, so had she made it up? But she still felt she was in pain, so I'm going to say no…

When they arrived at the station, Ben walked Kat down to the platform and carried her stuff, what a gentleman! Oh no, wait, no not really. After earlier, you cannot put Ben and gentleman in the same sentence. Unless you include a fully capitalised NOT. Her train arrived so he kissed her goodbye, she let him kiss her but she didn't kiss him back, she just couldn't. After what he did, he was in control, she was subservient, he could do and did do what he wanted, regardless of what she wanted. Goodbye mutuality…

When she arrived at home, she went downstairs to say hello to her parents, lied about how awful her weekend was, she just wasn't ready to get into it now, so she had a cigarette and went upstairs to her room. It was safer up there.

A few hours ago, Dominic had texted saying, *I hope your weekend is going better than your last few, it must be good to get away.*

She actually laughed at that, she thought about sending, yes get away from the shit show that is my home and into the arms of a rapist, oh joy! But she didn't send that, she didn't send anything. She couldn't…She just couldn't…

It was nowhere near her bedtime, but she wanted to cut, she was just casually doing her routine early. How organised! To say she was suicidal before was putting it lightly, no, she wasn't even suicidal now, she was just dead. So cut she did, it hurt, oh fuck, the rape hurt too, she wasn't ready for the similarity, so she threw her knife at the wall in front of her, she was done with it, she was done with everything.

The end.

No, not really the end, but do you like my change in font? Well, I do, so ha.

She picked up her knife, put it away, grabbed her laptop, got in bed and put on some music. It was then that she received a text from Ben, oh yeah, by the way, they were in a constant text conversation, but I had better things to do than mention it, sorry. It's not like any of it had any relevance to the story.

But here we go…

She then decided to check her texts, Ben said, *earlier felt so good jeez.*

Kat replied almost instantly after reading it, *Oh, I'm oh so glad it felt good for you, but maybe talk to your partner next time before trying something new?*

Are you OK? he replied almost instantly.

You hurt me. That reply made her start crying…

And you made me feel so good?

That's not how sex should work, is it? One person's pain should not make another person's pleasure.

Wait, should I be sorry? What a question to ask her, I don't think sorry is going to cut it, but your death might…

She sent him one word in the hopes that it would express everything she wanted to say *consent* is all she said. It's all she needed to say.

Consent? Don't give me that shit. You were asking for it.

Asking for it? I'm sorry, what planet is he living on? It was at that moment she started shaking in bed.

It was too early to go to sleep, even though she would give anything at that moment to not be conscious, but she was awake, unfortunately, so she put on a film on her laptop, in bed, zero fucks given to her homework, film was far more important anyway.

When the film was over, she sent Ben a four-character response, she was done with the conversation, no, she was done with him full stop.

Bye. Was all she said, four strong little characters, it was all she needed to say, she was nothing if not to the point.

In seconds he replied, even though she had left him hanging for a film amount of time.

Bye? So, is that it? I make a teeny mistake and you want to throw away two and a half years. Cheers.
Teeny? I feel violated.

I'll say sorry again.

OK, you didn't even properly say it the first time, but now all better.

Seriously? She didn't even grace that with a response, but she thought no, not all better you fucking retard, bye you cunt…

She just did the usual routine with her phone, put it away, with the alarm on and on charge. She just couldn't reply to Dominic at that moment in time because she knew it would end up with her, probably crying and talking about the joy that was her life and she just wasn't ready for that, but would she ever be ready? Probably not. She didn't even brush her teeth or cut, maybe she should get raped more often, no cutting was a positive, right?

She lay in bed, trying but failing to fall asleep for the longest time, her head was too busy overthinking to slumber. This day had been truly, beyond awful. Hashtag break-ups hurt. No, it was being raped that hurt…No, you know what, I didn't say that, I'm worried that the sheer mention of pain, rape or anything hurting will set her off crying again.

Oh shit, one sec, it's my manager.

'You do realise she can't hear you right?'

Oh shit, of course, I can say what I want.

What a fucking cunt for physically abusing her, I guess he's not smart enough to mentally abuse her. He deserves to hurt, hard.

OK, I'm back now…

Chapter 11

When she awoke for school the next day, her first thought was that she wished she didn't wake up at all, it was all too much. The idea of death was so much easier. So, like usual, she put her uniform on, went downstairs to go and have breakfast and then she got her coach. It was just her normal routine. Shame she didn't feel in any way normal…School went by in a blur, but not a fast blur, just a daze, she probably said a whopping ten words throughout the day, all in all, she didn't even go and get any lunch, she just chain-smoked on top of the Science Block. It was safer up there.

Ten minutes before the end of lunch Dominic appeared. 'Thought I'd find you here on the roof, hi.' He waved.

'Hi!' Kat laughed, she thought she'd escaped…

'Good weekend?'

'Well, I'm now single.'

'Oh shit, so no?'

'My choice.'

'Your choice maybe, but that doesn't mean you're good or at least, OK?'

She then kissed him, he was a straight male, so it must be what he wanted? She then moved on to tongues in her kisses.

Well, he seemed to be enjoying it…She moved her hands all over his body and he did the same for her.

She wanted, no needed to please him.

'Wait, are you sure?' Dominic stopped kissing her and asked.

'Do you not want to take me?'

'Um what a stupid question, of course I do, but you probably need to hear this…' He put a hand on her face and stroked it. 'There may be a chance I'm a virgin…'

'Bless! There's nothing to worry about. Take it slow, I'm right here.'

'Fuck me,' he said.

'Oh, don't you worry, I'm planning to,' Kat laughed the words out. 'OK, where?'

'Um, here?'

'My God, this roof has seen some action…'

He laughed. 'It certainly has…'

She answered by putting her lips on his, they then slowly but surely removed each other's clothes, there was a degree of passion in the way it was done.

I'm sorry Kat's not here right now. Can I take a message?

He entered her, they did it. Poof. Done. It could've been borderline romantic if Kat's head wasn't such a screwed-up mess.

'Happy?' Kat asked him after.

'Happy is putting it lightly.'

'You're welcome.'

He put his arms around her quite tightly. 'So, that was spontaneous for me, was that spontaneous for you?'

'I just want to make you happy; you deserve happiness.' I don't know about you, but I think that sounds like a rape thing…

'I think I love you.'

'No, you don't, I'm too fucked.'

'So am I, it's fine.'

'Ha, oh really? Are you? Were you anally raped yesterday too?'

Wait…?

What…?

Was all he could think.

'Wait? What? Why did we do that?'

'Wasn't it what you wanted?'

'Fuck.' He moved his arms away from her and put a hand on his mouth in shock.

'What?'

'Aw fuck, come here,' he put his arms around her again.

'What? I'm fine.'

He squeezed her in his arms. 'Shh, it's OK, I'm right here, no you're not…'

He was bang on the money because she started crying at that point.

'You fucker,' she said through tears, she couldn't stop them, she wished they weren't there. She felt like a baby.

'Where does he live? I'll go sort him out.'

'But it was me who fucked up taking your virginity. ME?'

'You've fucked nothing up, now give me his address, I want to fuck him up.'

'You'd do that?'

'Yes.'

'But he lives like two hours away?'

He started laughing. 'Regarde mon visage, regarde mon visage, je suis un bothered…' He pointed to his face and drew circles around it with his finger, then he borderline shouted, 'I AIN'T BOTHERED.' Little Britain joke, you either get it or you don't…

'Ha, so you can speak French and Spanish? What can't you do?'

'Rape someone, I don't think I could rape someone…'

But Kat made the decision to firmly ignore that. 'I think we've missed most of the afternoon's lessons…'

'That's fine. I have a journey to make anyway. Address?'

'Seriously?' She gave him the address.

'Yes, seriously, karma's a bitch I heard…'

'At least we don't have to worry about him moving out of this city suddenly, he's already far away…'

'I fucking love that you added to my Mod Sun reference there…' The reference is a song called *Karma* by Mod Sun…Listen…

'What can I say? I know my music…But it's not just getting the train, there will be a taxi ride from the station to his house?'

'Ah shit, sorry maybe next time, I'm scared of taxis.'

'Are you? Aw.'

'Note to self, Kat can make shitty jokes, but can't understand them.'

'Are you seriously going?'

'Don't miss me too much, I'll see you tomorrow.'

Just like that, he left.

Bye.

She did see him the next day, but not normally, not at school, in hospital…Her ex beat him up good and proper…He was fine, well, he was alive. She may have seen him, but didn't speak to him, he was unconscious. It wasn't exactly a friendly meeting between the two guys...There were no winners, just two losers. Remember, Ben was a rugby lad, so could fight. Dominic was luckily transferred to a hospital closer to home, so Kat could see him without seeing the rapist, but she would've happily travelled further. Distance didn't matter.

She was still there the next day, she hadn't gone home, she had slept there, it was only him that mattered, not school. Kat sat in his hospital room and held his hand, he was passed out, his face was all messed up with bruises.

When all of a sudden, he came to, in panic, it was a very abrupt awakening, he even used his fists to defend himself. He thought he was still in the fight, so he thought he needed fists, then he looked around and put his fists down.

'No, shh, I'm right here.' She tried to calm him down.

'W-w-where am I? What day is it?'

'School let me know you were here on Tuesday, thank God they know we're buddies, well, we hang out enough...I've just been sat here, no school, hey maybe you should get injured more often,' she laughed. 'Not going to school is great, but don't worry me so much next time, yeah? But it's Wednesday now.'

'Shit.'

'Yes, shit, you really scared me.'

'How are you?'

She laughed at that. 'You're in a hospital bed, how can you ask me that? The real question is how are you?'

'Because I know you've been through it, what's a few bruises in comparison?'

'My God, that's an almighty bruise if it knocked you out…'

'So, answer me, how are you?'

'I honestly don't know how to answer that.'

'En Español?'

Kat let out a big laugh.

'When can I leave here?' he asked seriously.

'Hopefully, soon, I think they were just waiting for you to wake up, so should be soon.'

'Today?'

'Do I look like a doctor?'

'Yes, but not your conventional doctor, a witch doctor.'

She just hit him in response to that.

A Nurse then came into his room to check on him.

'Ah! Good! You're awake! Are you hungry? Shall I get you some food?'

'Can I leave?'

'I think the doctor will want to keep you for another night.'

'Fuck.'

'So, food?'

'I guess so…'

So the Nurse left the room, went to go grab a tray of food and put it in front of him, she checked the machine he was connected to, filled in some sheets and left.

He tucked in, he needed energy, so he ate fairly quickly.

'Why do I have to wait? I'm ready to leave now?'

'Sorry, I think I trust the doctors more on this, what with their years in med school…'

'Again, I say fuck.'

'Serious conversation time?' Kat asked.

'We weren't exactly having a jovial conversation, but OK…'

'Are you my boyfriend now?'

Dominic breathed in and out a few times at that question before answering, as if thinking of a suitable response, but answer it he did.

'I would love to be,' he grabbed and held on to her hand. 'Fuck, I would love to be,' he enlaced their fingers, 'but I think you need time on your own to heal.'

Tears formed in her eyes. 'Is it because I'm too much of a mess?'

'What? No?'

She moved her hand away from his, stood up and went home, she felt she needed to get out of there…

Going home cleared her head, surprisingly. When she came back to the hospital the next day, Dominic was getting ready to leave. If he wasn't going to school, then there was no way in hell she was going.

'I think my parents want to pick me up, but I kind of want to go out.'

'Go out? But where?'

'Here's a crazy idea, the zoo?'

Kat just laughed. 'What about your parents?'

In one minute, he showed Kat his phone, he had just sent a text to his mum. It said *going to the zoo to celebrate getting out of hospital, see you later!*

'All done! Let's go, thank God I packed light.'

'I have no words…'

'Good! Then be quiet.'

They then walked to the Reception, well, Dominic practically ran, when they arrived there Dominic asked for signing out paperwork, a Receptionist asked no questions and gave it to him. He fiercely started filling it in.

'Wait, where are your parents?' the Receptionist eventually asked.

'In the car, outside,' Dominic said, lying without hesitation, I like it. The paperwork was now done, so he handed it back to the Receptionist.

She started looking through it and said, 'Can I help you with anything else today?' She looked up as she said the last word, only to see Kat and Dominic about to go through the exit.

When they left, Dominic knelt and kissed the ground 'now, let's go celebrate my freedom by going to visit some animals who weren't quite so lucky in the freedom department.'

'Well, that's one way to describe a zoo...' Kat said.

So, they went to a zoo, according to Kat's phone there was one only about ten minutes away on the bus, so they went there via bus, while they were waiting for it Kat had a smoke.

Quite soon they got to the zoo, bought tickets and entered.

The first exhibit they got to see had gophers in it and there was a little disabled one who the others had to help feed.

'Aw, that's so sweet!' Kat exclaimed about the gophers.

'Sweet, maybe. Drag, yes.'

'Drag? Seriously? He just needs extra help? I could probably do with extra help, does that make me a drag? Just let the gophers be sweet...Bye.' She started walking towards the exit, she may have taken that far too personally...

'Where are you going? Survival of the Fittest?' He grabbed her by the arm.

'Home. Just let the animals be sweet.' She pulled her arm away from his and left and that concluded their first date if it was even a date…?

Dominic may have been allowed to leave hospital on the Thursday, you know the day after Wednesday, but he wasn't actually in school until Friday.

Kat tried to avoid him all day, but especially at lunch, but unfortunately for her, he knew exactly where she had gone because she wasn't eating, she needed something to suppress her appetite, so cigarettes it was. Tasty!

He stepped onto the roof and said, 'Can we talk?'

Chapter 12

'Do I even have a choice?'

'Not really, no.'

So, she took a big drag, ha drag, of her cigarette and breathed it out, relaxing time was over, so she stared at him, folded her arms over her chest and waited for him to speak.

'I know your hiding place now…So, ha…But I need you in my life, come back.' He sat down next to her and put her hand in his.

'I'm sorry. Upon thinking about it, I'm not ready to be some one-night stand and can't you admit what you said was wrong?'

'You're not. Oh, my good God, you're not, I meant it when I said I think I love you, actually no I don't think I love you, I do love you. I definitely don't just want you, it's more than that. For you, I'll admit what I said was wrong, I need you. Do you have any idea how hard this is for me?'

'You what?' She wiped the tears from her eyes that had now magically appeared.

He put his face so it was facing hers, but didn't kiss her. 'I, Dominic, am in love with you, Kat, but I just think you need time to heal.' He started laughing 'well, your ex certainly needs time to heal, I got him pretty good.'

'How can you make jokes in regards to something so serious?'

'It's a talent I'm quite proud of.'

'Can you be my friend then? While I'm healing?'

'Just because I think it's wise we don't get in a relationship now, doesn't mean I don't want a relationship with you whatsoever. So, of course, I'll be your friend.'

'How long?'

'Fuck knows, I'm not going to put a time stamp on it, it'll happen when it happens, just focus on getting better.'

'Do you…Um…Want me…?'

'That's such a stupid question, just know that.'

'So answer it?'

'I have a feeling I'm really going to regret this, but we've already slept together up here, so I'm just going to blame the roof.'

In answer, he kissed her.

'Sort out my shit? Then kisses can happen regularly?' Kat asked.

'I hope you're not taking me saying wait as sort your shit out?'

She laughed. 'Well, actually…'

So he kissed her again.

'So, it's Friday and you're going home, how do you feel about that?'

'If I'm honest, mixed.'

'No shit, shall we go get some lunch?'

'OK.'

The rest of the school day was quite normal for Kat, she didn't feel happy after her conversation with Dominic, but she felt happier, not so unwanted. Like normal she got her coach home. Shame when she got home it wasn't normal, it almost seemed like her parents were waiting for her to get home, so they could talk.

Her father spoke, 'Sit, let's talk.'

'Very formal, should I be worried?' YES, YOU SHOULD.

'Just sit...'

'Um OK.' So she sat and started rolling herself a cigarette.

'So I spoke to Ben's dad on the phone today...' The very mention of the name Ben stopped her from rolling. 'I know you broke up with him, so it's OK if you don't know, but Ben is apparently nursing some pretty serious physical injuries at the moment from a fight. Hey, wait didn't you go to hospital earlier this week because your friend got in a fight? Know anything about that?'

Fuck.

She couldn't even speak, she just started crying.

Her mother stopped staring at her computer, looked at her daughter and said, 'If you know anything, please tell us.'

Kat's tears were now flowing more strongly, she was a mess, this was a mess or at least an awful situation.

The father then said, 'I'm going to take your tears to mean that they are related, are they related? Why?'

Kat just about nodded.

'OK, so why?' the father asked.

Kat's mouth still wasn't working, it was such a difficult four-letter word to say. Rapture was as close as she could get, but it's not like she randomly said rapture. Her life may have been crazy but all her mental marbles were still intact.

'Talk to me, I haven't got all day.' Wrong thing to say, oh I'm sorry if your daughter struggling to speak is an inconvenience for you.

'I can't say it.'

'Yes, you can. We're here to help.' Help and sniff, don't forget about sniff…

'OK, fine, here goes…' She tried to steady her breathing, but she failed miserably. 'My friend went to go beat him up,' she knew how she wanted to finish her sentence, but actually doing it was a whole other thing…

'Was there a reason?'

'Obviously.'

'Care to share?'

That's where it got difficult for her. Like ridiculously difficult.

Without meaning to, she lowered the volume of her voice, it came out as barely a whisper, 'Because he anally raped me.'

'Sorry, what was that?'

Her voice was still quiet, but audible, 'Because he anally raped me.'

'WHAT? ARE YOU SURE?' he raised his voice.

She should've answered yes, I'm pretty sure, I was there after all, but she didn't. Her answer was merely a nod.

'Fuck, no shit you broke up with him.'

She had gone back to non-verbal answers, so she nodded again.

'Games to take your mind off it?' Notice how he hasn't asked the humble question of are you OK and the mother hasn't said anything. Not a word, surely work isn't that interesting? It's not like she was deaf. Also notice how mentioning going to the police hasn't been mentioned either, playing games is far more important.

'If by that, what you really mean is taking cocaine, let me eat something first, I'm starving, I missed lunch.'

'Yeah, sure or we could have an early dinner?'

'I vote dinner.'

'I don't think your mother has taken anything out of the freezer to defrost, so freezer food or takeaway?'

'I'm obviously going to vote takeaway.'

'Then get a menu out so we can order?'

'Yes, sir!' She saluted and got a menu out. Tonight she had voted for Chinese. So she got the Chinese menu out and passed it to her mother.

The mother then spoke, I love how food gets her to speak, but the fact that her daughter was anally raped doesn't. She has got her priorities in order... 'Why do we even use menus? We get the same thing every time?'

'Shall I just order then?' Kat asked.

'Yes, maybe,' the father said.

So Kat called them and ordered, the Chinese was only a few minutes' walk away, so she would go and collect it later. 'Should be about half an hour,' she said after she had ordered and hung up the phone, so she put the menu away.

So until she had to leave, she watched TV, while her parents worked, half an hour passed quick enough. When it had, she stood up, got ready to leave and left. She felt like a robot, just completing tasks for the fuck of it, with no emotion, emphasis on no emotion. Maybe Dominic was right, she was a drag, she couldn't even look after herself, let alone anyone else, so relationships were out of the question.

She arrived at the Chinese takeaway, but first went into the newsagents next door to buy some tobacco, they never asked her for an ID so she was able to buy some. Before buying and asking for tobacco she looked around, who knows why the thought popped into her head, but it did, I guess zero fucks were given to life now or anything at all, she needed to get some excitement in her life and I guess she saw shoplifting as a way to get that excitement or at least a way to get free stuff…

Hmm, what did she want, what did she want? She decided on a bag of sweets, something small that would easily be hidden and something she could eat and enjoy. So she hid them in a pocket and walked over to the checkout to buy tobacco. It only went and fucking worked! Tobacco was acquired and so was a bag of sweets! That's a lot of oral pleasure…She only went and jumped for joy when she left the shop, walked a few paces so she was out of sight of the shopkeeper and placed a sweet into her mouth.

She then went inside the Chinese to collect her food, she paid for it with her mum's bank card and all was done and dusted, so she embarked on the short walk back home. She probably only took about ten minutes all in all, but when she went back downstairs, all hell had broken loose.

'We've started. Here you go. Couldn't wait, it was all just too much.' Oh, I'm sorry, too much for you? Try putting yourself in Kat's shoes. Her father put a single line of cocaine on a mirror with the usual straw, in front of the chair she normally sat at, at the table. I think it's safe to say she had missed lunch, would start on the cocaine and miss dinner and would probably miss breakfast by waking up too late. Ladies and gentlemen that makes a hat-trick!

So, she came to the conclusion, if you can't beat them, join them.

She took the line. Because she was just a fucked up, raped druggie, it was all she was good for. It made her feel awake, how irritating, given how she just wanted to sleep, preferably forever.

'Game?' the father asked.

Kat started laughing. 'No, you've just had some go faster juice, it's the perfect time to work, is it not?'

'I'll take that as a yes then…Go on, be a good girl and get the Poker out.'

The new normal then resumed, with lines aplenty and Poker, a most wonderful pairing!

But tonight, it was Kat who left first and went up to bed, how unusual, she just needed some time alone, to take a breather.

She didn't go up to her room to sleep, she went up to cry, she collapsed on her floor by the door to do so, she needed physical pain to try and combat the mental pain. So she took her knife out and cut herself whilst crying, her wrist was such a mess, shame she didn't care, remotely. The cutting helped to calm her down, it didn't fully calm her down, well, she was still crying.

She didn't even check her phone to check her texts after or put it on charge, just nothing, the cutting took long enough to warrant going to bed after. So she did just that. How peaceful! But no not really…

Her Saturday was typical, in the day and in the night, but with more food than the day before, when they were playing Poker in the evening, by the way, playing Poker now only happened with cocaine, but the father decided to speak.

'By the way, if what you're saying is true,' yes because people often lie about being raped? It's a common occurrence? 'But I've cut off all contact with Ben's dad, please don't be lying.' He took another line, the cocaine was downstairs again tonight, not upstairs, where would it be next time?

Everest? The possibilities were endless...

After taking his line, it was time for Kat and her mother to take theirs.

Kat felt fake sympathy for her father, aw he lost a friend. Poor thing! Well, she lost her life? OK, that may be a slight exaggeration, but that's how it felt...

Once again Kat went up to her room before her parents went to theirs, notice how I didn't say she went to bed. It was by no means early just earlier than her parents went up so she should've gone straight to bed. But instead, she cut herself, it was the only shred of normality left in her life, then, as per, aside from the last day or so, she actually checked the texts on her phone that night, as per, she had received quite a few messages from, you guessed it, Dominic.

He basically wanted to know if she was OK, well, the answer to that was no and to let her know that he cared. How sweet! Shame she didn't reply, but if she had she would've probably said something like...Don't feel like you need to text me all the time, friends don't text all the time...I'm fine.

She then went to bed, sleep just didn't come as naturally to her as it used to, so she just laid there for hours, but eventually, after hours, she fell asleep.

When she awoke on the Sunday, that was it she had given up. Done. Complete.

Bye.

Before getting up, she just laid in bed doing nothing, for hours, but she eventually went on her phone and ignoring all his previous messages typed Dominic a message *Parents now know. Help.*

She then went on her laptop to watch something because she was bored and he didn't reply straight away, she was hungry, but felt sick, so food was a no-go. At long last, he replied, with a casual *fuck.* Yes, fuck indeed. She had nothing to say to that, so she didn't reply and said nothing at all.

The rest of her Sunday consisted of watching TV downstairs, eating food and not texting Dominic, in the early evening she went up to her room to relax and he decided to call her almost as soon as she got up there.

She, mind you, not happily, answered it.

The first word that was said was just him repeating his text 'fuck,' was all he said.

She made herself laugh with her reply, to Eminem's Lose Yourself she sang or said, it's a rap song so I don't know…But she spoke the words 'snap back to reality, watch your profanity.' If you've not seen it, I strongly advise you to type sNaPbAcKtOrEaLiTy into YouTube, go, now.

'No, be serious, are you even vaguely, OK?'

She just started crying, 'They know.'

'Oh gosh, I know they do, did they help at all?'

'No,' the crying was proper, she had to blow her nose. 'Cocaine just keeps you awake and I just want to sleep forever.'

'My poor little baby, you can talk to me about anything, I'm right here.'

'No, no, I'm fine.'

'Don't give me that shit.'

'But I'm fine?'

'Don't lie to me.'

'But it makes your life easier if I do?'

'Oh, my bad, I forgot this was all about me?'

She couldn't reply to that, she couldn't speak, so she just hung up the call. Bye, boy!

She just watched something shitty on her laptop, when about half an hour in, she received a text from, oh I'm not even going to say who from. Go on take a wild guess…

But he said *just know I'm here for you, it may not be much but I care so much about you. You can hang up the call, that's fine, but just know I'm not going anywhere. You're in control you can talk to me if or when you want, you can't hang me up, well, you can on a washing line or something, but please don't…*

It was when he mentioned control that it got her crying again. In all other aspects, her control had been taken away from her, whether that was Ben or parents and he was just giving it to her. I'm sorry what? She couldn't even reply, what would she even say? Um, cheers?

She just watched stuff on her laptop until she thought it was late enough to go to bed, she underwent her normal routine of brushing her teeth, phone and cutting. Again, it took her quite a while to fall asleep, she should really lose some brain cells and stop thinking so much. If only it were that easy…

Chapter 13

When she awoke the next day, she undertook her normal school routine of getting dressed, breakfast and coach. Shame it was only her routine that was normal and not her. She couldn't even really eat her cereal, she just couldn't, she made it like normal but didn't eat it like normal. She just felt sick all the time. She maybe ate half of it and even that was hard.

When she got to school was when her mind thought of all the homework she hadn't done, but did she care? No, not in the slightest. Her morning lessons were dull, she was just waiting for it to get to break, she was just waiting for when she could go for a smoke. Then the bell finally rang to signify the start of break. So she went to her special smoking place, rolled, lit up and took a drag, she stared at her cigarette and wished she could evaporate like the smoke.

Within minutes Dominic appeared.

'You're so predictable.' He laughed.

'Hey, it's called an addiction, leave me be...' She cowered her head.

He went to go sit next to her 'never.'

'Sorry for not replying to your text yesterday, by the way, I did get it but you saying you were giving me control got to me, like in all other aspects of my life, my control has been taken from me, so thank you.'

'Any time, future girlfriend.'

She hit him at that and he just laughed, he loved her, oh boy, did he love her, but she was shit at violence.

'So how are you? Let's not talk about the trials and tribulations that is my life today. Let's talk about you.'

'Ha, are you OK? But you love talking about you?' That cheeky bastard, but he wished he could kiss her, so he was sweet and sour...A sugar-coated potato? Oh, I don't know or maybe sweet and sour sauce makes more sense? Oh, what do you put on your chips? Ketchup? Mayonnaise? No, neither, sugar.

She just hit him again at what he said, there was a theme occurring here with violence, well, more specifically hitting Dominic, violence is too general, but she also laughed. He cradled his shoulder as if he was in pain where she hit him as if to invoke some sympathy that he wasn't going to get especially as he also started laughing.

He took a minute to think of what to say because her reply had been violence, then he said it, he only went and bloody said it, control my ass.

'You know what I'm OK, I'm actually OK for once, when I say that it's normally a lie. But I think I'm getting there, I've started my therapy and it's actually going OK, I was expecting much worse, like much, much worse, I thought it would be awful, but it's not, it may sound stupid, no it definitely sounds stupid but I don't care, why should I? I'm talking to you, you get it, but she's an actual person, not a shrink. Well, anyway I think it's helping or at least will help. Hey, she started me on these Vitamin C pills for happiness, they're subtle, but I think they help a bit, would you like to try?'

'Vitamin C? Are you sure?'

'Quite sure yeah, just try it, it's not going to hurt.'

She gave a reluctant 'OK.'

'Sweet.'

He pulled out a tin of pills, they weren't even labelled, good thing too, if they were labelled she wouldn't of touched them, they were just in a tin from home wrapped up in a sheath topped with foil, the tray they came in, he pulled two out, one for each of them, good thing Dominic brought a water bottle. Was he planning this?

'Bottoms up,' Dominic said, they then put them in their mouths and swallowed. Pills, what a nice way to finish break.

Until lunchtime Kat tried to notice differences in her mood from the pill but couldn't, none at all. She assumed it was probably because they were plant-based, but no, she just needed more, one dose wasn't going to do it.

Then it got to lunchtime, she was actually feeling hot food today, not just a sandwich, so she got herself a tray of hot food and went to sit opposite Dominic, who was having a sandwich. I'm sorry, is this role reversal?

Before she had fully settled down and started her food, Dominic said, 'Pill?'

'Ecstasy? But we're in school?'

'Glad to see even through all the shit you're going through, your sense of humour is still questionable, needs help and hasn't changed.'

'Stop being so mean to me.'

'But you love it, pain is the new pleasure after all.' Wrong, WRONG thing to say, stupid, stupid boy…

Just the sheer mention of pain got Kat crying, she stopped eating and wiped her eyes on her sleeves.

'Fuck. Did I say something wrong?'

'No, no, I just got something in my eye.' Yes, you said something wrong, was there any real need to mention pain?

'Hmm…Not sure if I believe you, but OK, pill?'

'OK, but I think just taking it just makes you think it works, I felt nothing after the first one. A placebo.'

'Duly noted, Dr Kat, just give it time, they help me, so why not you? Just try and believe in it yeah, for me?'

She started laughing. 'So is Holland & Barratt your new drug dealer?' Holland & Barratt is a shop that mainly sells plant-based medicines…

'Don't make me comment on your humour again.' He stood up and shouted, 'HOLD ME BACK, I'M WARNING YOU, I'LL DO IT.'

'Just shut up and give me the pill, you're lucky I like drugs.'

He did as he was told, they once again took a pill each, together. Bottoms up!

They both, then went back to their lunches, Kat started to feel strange, but she tried to ignore it. They continued sitting there until ten minutes before the end of lunch, she wanted to go for a typical cigarette, so Dominic went with her.

She didn't even make it to the bottom of the Science Block when multiple seizures for Kat had started to take place outside of it. Dominic more than panicked, he freaked the fuck out, he held Kat's shaking body in his arms, getting help from a teacher meant leaving her side and he just couldn't do that. Some younger pupils then walked past, who Dominic didn't know, but they went to go get a teacher, to help, it was obvious and quite clear she needed help.

'What's going on? I'm confused, what's going on? Am I OK?' Kat asked Dominic from down on the floor.

'Yes, shh, you're fine, I'm right here, I've got you…' It was at that moment, Dominic started crying, he tried but failed to hide his tears from Kat.

That concluded their conversation for now because she started convulsing again, yes, that's right, more seizures.

A teacher then arrived. 'Oh fuck, they weren't joking.'

'WHAT DO I DO?' Dominic practically screamed the words out.

'Just hold her, it's all you can do, let me call an ambulance.'

'OK, fine and maybe get a bloody Biology teacher in this situation. I don't exactly need to know where the Equator is,' he said this because she taught Geography.

'Yes, of course,' was all she said.

But first, the teacher didn't move but she called an ambulance instead and Dominic just held Kat's shaking body, it was all he could do.

'They're on their way, hopefully fifteen minutes. I said it was urgent…' she said and then ran off to get a Biology teacher.

It was at that moment, Kat came out of unconsciousness, she asked the same questions as she had before, but only once this time, 'What's going on? Am I OK?'

Dominic laughed and basically cried out his response, he was just happy she was conscious, 'No, you're Kat, who the fuck is, OK?'

'Oh, I'm sorry, I forgot you were a comedian,' she said very weakly and turned her head away from his and shut her eyes as if she wanted to go to sleep, well, she had just had multiple seizures, so I think we can forgive her for not sounding strong or being wide awake.

It didn't take her very long at all to fall asleep, Dominic just held her in his arms. The Geography teacher then came back with not just a Biology teacher, but a Nurse as well. They both looked at her, then Dominic said quite quietly, so as not to wake her, 'She has luckily fallen asleep, my God that was scary.'

It was the Nurse who spoke first, 'I saw nothing, but judging by what I was told, you were more than brave.' The teachers just nodded.

Dominic then attempted but failed to stop crying, he didn't give a shit if he was being a baby, but he needed answers, 'What could even have caused it?'

The Nurse again was the one to speak, 'Many things…head trauma, infections and drugs to name but a few.'

'Drugs?'

'Yes, Seizures are a common complication of drug intoxication.'

'So, like illegal drugs?'

'No, like antidepressants, stimulants and antihistamines.'

Ha upon hearing that, I think Dominic knows he made a mistake, no, not just a mistake, but a fuck up, an almighty fuck up. He started crying again, his eyes were still wet from his last batch of tears but now they were being cleaned away with fresh tears.

But he didn't give her stimulants or antihistamines? No, he didn't…

But Vitamin C is not an antidepressant?

No, it's not, but maybe he lied...?

Oh shit, maybe he lied!

'No, now's the time to stop crying, she's asleep, she's stopped seizing.' The Biology teacher said, he finally spoke!

Two Paramedics armed with a stretcher, well, it was more like a hospital bed, it's not like she was dead...Yet...But her condition was quite serious. But they then turned the corner and walked towards them with a Receptionist...

'OK, it was a good idea telling a Receptionist where we were,' the Nurse said to the Geography teacher.

The Paramedics then practically ripped Kat out of Dominic's arms and put her on the bed, they took her stats and instead of holding all of her, Dominic just held her hand. Everything seemed OK with her stats, so a Paramedic asked, 'Is anyone coming with her?'

'I am,' Dominic said straight away.

'Um no you're not, you can't just leave, you've got school...' the Geography teacher said all high and mightily.

He let go of Kat's arm, turned to the Geography teacher and turned his hand around in small circles around his other hand and slowly put up his middle finger on his other hand.

The Geography teacher just stared, well, that shut her up.

The Nurse couldn't help but laugh, she then said to the Geography teacher, 'I think that told you.'

Dominic just poured all his attention back onto Kat and went back to holding her hand, he was very serious about what he just did, he didn't understand why the Nurse was laughing.

'Can I help at all?' Dominic asked the Paramedics.

'No, don't worry, lad, just come with us, if you're coming?' one of the Paramedics said and looked at the teachers for help. They said nothing, the only help they got was the Geography teacher motioning for them to go with her hand.

'OK, cool, let's go,' the other Paramedic said.

The teachers stayed where they were and Dominic went with Kat, on a merry journey to hospital, he would go anywhere with her, he loved her but he knew he had fucked up. He quite clearly had seriously fucked up. Yes, he may very well have been trying to help, but multiple seizures say otherwise…He didn't help at all.

When they were all in the ambulance, but before they set off Dominic started full frontal weeping again and said, 'Fuck. I think I fucked up.'

'Shh, no you didn't, you've done perfectly,' one of the Paramedics said.

'Yes or no, can antidepressants cause seizures?'

'It's not common, but yes, they can, through an allergy,' the same Paramedic said. 'Do you think that's what caused this…?'

Dominic put his head in his hands. 'Oh, dear Christ, then, to put it bluntly, I think I most definitely fucked up…'

'Sorry? You need to explain more, I'm lost.'

'I lied. I thought they would help, not hurt her, I only wanted to help her.'

'Wait, did you drug her? Without her knowing? Without consent?'

'Fuck. Don't say it like that.'

'I'm just going to say you're lucky we aren't cops because that sounds illegal…'

'Illegal? Fuck…I only wanted to help…'

'Yes, fuck indeed, the fact that you're so visibly upset is a good thing too.'

'Ha, lucky tears?'

'Something like that…'

Nothing else was said, nothing else needed to be said. It wasn't too long a journey to the hospital, so they got there in good time, but it wasn't exactly a happy visit. They quickly unloaded themselves from the ambulance, Kat was given a room and that was it.

Being unconscious in a hospital bed made Kat look so frail.

Dominic could only do one thing and one thing only, blame himself…

Chapter 14

When Kat came to, she felt rather strange, not like herself at all. It seemed she was in a hospital room, in a hospital bed, but why? She had no memory. She tried to get up but couldn't. Her parents were there and were pacing around nervously. Wait, her parents were there? What the fuck happened?

'Oh shit, you're awake. Hello, darling. How are you feeling? Get the doctor, he said to get him when she was awake,' the father looked and said to the mother, then went back to looking at his daughter.

'I'm feeling confused.'

'So are we, but don't worry I'm sure the doctor will fill us in.'

'What even happened?'

'Dominic said you had multiple seizures.'

'Dominic?' His mere name brought out a smile from her.

'Yeah, he's right outside, he only left because we wanted some private family time…Not because he wanted to.'

'Aw, that's so fucking sweet.' Sweet? Just you wait until you hear what happened, you won't be saying that for much longer…

'Is he your boyfriend?'

Kat laughed at the question, 'not yet,' was all she said.

The mother then entered back into the room with a doctor.

'Hello, how are you doing? You've been through quite the ordeal...'

He pulled a chair up to her bed and sat in it.

'I'm quite impressed, knowing you were depressed,' he then uncovered her wrist so it was just on show, her dad gasped at the sight of it whereas the mother just fainted, so Kat covered her wrist up and glared at the doctor. 'But knowing and trying to fix it yourself is impressive, but unfortunately, you're allergic.'

She laughed. 'To what? Vitamin C?'

'No, to the antidepressants you were on?'

Antidepressants? What? What the actual fuck? But then she thought about it. Then she really thought about it. There was only one possible explanation. Her being in hospital was his fault. Her internal monologue went back and forth between angry and upset, she felt abused, yes, being raped was abuse, but this was something else...If he was outside, she needed to talk to him, she needed to hear it from him.

'Oh, yes, of course, bugger.'

Her mother then came to and stood up. She then started crying and grabbed Kat's wrist. 'Why didn't you tell us?'

'Maybe just maybe, I didn't fancy sharing everything with you?'

'It looks so painful, why?'

Kat started crying, 'I'm not even going to answer that...'

'But why not? If we're being all honest now?'

'Yes, but not out of choice. Choice is the key word here; the honesty has been raped out of me and I'm allowed to say that...'

The mother and father both started crying at that. Choice was the keyword there. She didn't choose to have her wrist put on show. She didn't choose to have antidepressants; she was lied to…Kat joined in with the tears.

'I don't know where you got them from but I commend you, it's so hard to be a teen these days…' the doctor commented.

'Just be quiet, stick to your medicines, it's what your good at and we'll stick to our daughter,' the father said. But they weren't exactly good with their daughter? The one guy who was (notice how I said was, so past tense) but he's outside.

'Do you three mind leaving and sending Dominic in please?' Kat asked, she may not have been ready to see him, but she had to see him…

'Yes, of course,' the mother said and went over to hug her, then they left her room, asked Dominic to go inside and left the kids to it.

Dominic nervously and timidly walked into her room, focusing on one foot in front of the other, he was worried she knew, how could he not be? He felt small, so he tried to make himself look small, he was bent over, they both knew what was up, but who would speak first? I'll give you a hint, it wasn't Dominic.

'What the actual fuck did you give me? Jeez because I never knew oranges could cause multiple seizures, vitamin C my ass…' She then started crying, 'Haven't I been through enough shit? I TRUSTED YOU.'

'I'm so sorry but sorry is not a big enough word for what I feel…' He put his hand and held onto hers tightly, but she didn't hold it back, she just kept her hand clutched into a fist on the hospital bed.

'Apparently, I had an allergic reaction to the antidepressants I was on, do you know anything about that?'

'Fuck,' he practically shouted.

'Is not a big enough word…'

'I was only trying to help…'

'Maybe, just maybe, next time try talking to me before drugging me? Oh, and what about choice? You've emotionally raped me.' She crossed her arms; she couldn't even have Dominic touching her.

'I don't want to leave, but do you want me to leave?'

'My parents now know about my wrist and have seen it, so cheers for that…' It was at that point Dominic started crying. He put his arms around her but she moved them away with anger, it was all too much.

She was done talking to him, so she said no more.

'But I…I love you.'

Silence. She couldn't even look at him anymore, so she looked at the tree outside, it was much more interesting…

'Shall I go?'

Again silence. He took that as an answer that yes, he should go, so he stood up and left her hospital room.

He left the hospital and, on the way, out, waved goodbye to her parents. Well, her father, who knows where the mother was.

'Are you OK? You're crying?' he asked.

'Yeah, yeah, I'm fine, it's just awful seeing her like that.'

'Oh God, we know, but at least she'll get better.' He started laughing. 'Shame she didn't have an allergic reaction to anything illegal she took.'

'I don't know why you're laughing; you would hate that too.'

'I'm sorry?'

'Oh, don't you worry, I know the truth,' and he put a finger over one of his nostrils and breathed in a fat line of air.

Well, that shut the father up, so Dominic went outside, if Kat was upset with him, that was one thing, but if she didn't even want to be friends with him anymore, it was understandable, but a whole other thing. He stared up at all the roofs he walked past and thought about jumping. Jumping? It would be so easy. Poof. Gone. Goodnight world. But no, that was selfish. She may be upset with him, but he knew even she didn't wish he was dead and he just couldn't upset her anymore. He couldn't do that to her, he had done quite enough, already.

So, he just walked around the block and went back into hospital. He went back to Kat's room, where her parents now were. He walked in.

'Sorry guys, do you mind leaving, we're talking,' Kat said.

'So what? You can tell him more family secrets?' the father basically shouted the words out, then he left.

The mother then scrambled after him and said, 'Who knows what that was about, let me just go see what's up with him…'

'You hate me, your father hates me, hmm, I wonder what I can do to make your mum hate me?'

'Wait, what did you do to my dad? And I don't hate you, I'm just pissed off.' She started laughing. 'You're such a drama queen.'

'I'm genuinely so sorry.'

She kept the laughter going. 'And so you should be, you could've at least given me some fun drugs?'

'Next time I will.' He started laughing but then stopped abruptly. 'No next time, there won't be a next time.'

She kept laughing. 'No, you were so close, just kill me next time!'

'Wait. Fuck. Did you nearly die?'

'You of all people should know my humour is fucked, but no I don't think I was close, unfortunately…'

'How are you feeling?'

'Like I'm desperate for a fag.'

'In my expert opinion, I'd say let's go.'

'Expert?'

'I didn't say what I was an expert in…'

She laughed, she did love him and his sense of humour, deep down, deep, deep down, 'OK and what are you an expert in?'

He started laughing. 'Umm, the TV show *Two and a Half Men*…'

Kat chuckled again. 'Has it helped you in life so far?'

'Charlie Sheen, yes; Ashton Kutcher not so much.' You either get that joke or you don't…I'm not going to explain it…

They then got themselves ready and left her room, they had a quest. When they left her room only the mother was outside, the father had gone walkabout.

'Where do you think you're going?' the mother asked.

'Can I please have one of your cigarettes?'

'For fucks sake, I suppose so.'

'Appreciated.' So her mother took out her box of cigarettes, took one out and gave it to her daughter along with a lighter.

Kat and Dominic then went outside, when they were out, Kat lit the cigarette and just stared at it, she was in pure bliss...

She eventually spoke to Dominic, 'So, tell me, what did you do to my dad? Why does he seemingly hate you?'

He laughed, hard. 'He may know that I know.' He tried and failed to regain composure. 'Haha I may have done this to him,' once again he put a finger over one of his nostrils and breathed in a fat line of air.

'Oh my God, you've got some serious balls to do that, but that's fucking hilarious,' Kat stated and said it through laughter.

'Does that mean my sense of humour is good?'

'Don't push it...'

She finished her cigarette fairly quickly, so they went back to her room and she got back in bed, what a good little patient she was. Kat's father had returned and was sitting outside with her mother. Dominic was just happy to be with a non-seizing Kat, so he joined her in her room and stayed there.

Dominic then said, 'OK, I'm so done with waiting, I can't do it anymore, come here.' He practically jumped into her bed and put his arms around her.

Kat pushed him away slightly and said, 'Wait, does this mean I have a boyfriend?' She whispered the last part, 'Am I taken?'

'If you want to be,' he stated.

She laughed. 'Let me think about that for a moment.'

She tried to look pensive as if she was thinking and came to the conclusion to kiss him. 'That's my answer,' she stated.

He just lay in bed with her and kept his arms firmly around her, she liked the feeling. They didn't go to sleep, but they closed their eyes, they felt calm, great and at peace, Kat would trade death for this any day.

'I think I love you,' Kat said to Dominic.

'Think? Well, I do love you, so I win, so ha.'

Kat and Dominic both opened their eyes and stared at each other, there was nothing else to look at. No more words were said, no more words needed to be said, staring was the only conversation they needed.

Then, all of a sudden, the doctor came in with both her parents, he walked over to the full bed and stood over it.

'How do you feel? I think you may be ready to leave us.'

Kat sat up so vigorously at that, that she knocked Dominic off the bed, it may have hurt him, but she didn't care, 'really?'

'Ow?'

But she ignored him, in fact everyone ignored him…

'Yes, really,' the doctor said.

Kat shook her fists in front of her in joy at the thought.

'But I think you need therapy, so that's my prescription to you, I've already spoken to the therapists here about it, three days' time, here.'

Dominic, at that moment, stood up and said, 'Don't worry, doc, I'll make sure she goes, if it helps me, it should help her.'

'Thank you,' the doctor said, 'and remember, Kat, it may be, no it will be scary at first, but it should help in the long run.'

But Kat wasn't really listening, she was just ready to leave.

As if the doctor said nothing, Kat said, 'If I'm allowed to leave hospital, please leave my room so I can get dressed.'

'Of course, and don't hesitate to pop your head into my office when you come in for your therapy,' the doctor said. Hmm, I don't know about you, but I think he might have said that because he doesn't trust her to go. But they all left and Kat stripped off the hospital gown, found her uniform and put it back on.

She was ready.

Well, as ready as she would ever be…

So she left her room and said to her parents, 'Lego.'

Dominic laughed.

'I'm sorry? What? Do you want some Lego?' the mother asked.

Kat joined in with Dominic's laughter. 'No,' her laughter was strong. 'It means let's go.'

'Oh right, yes, of course, let's, Dominic, I think the very least we can do is offer you a ride to your home?'

'No, I should be fine on public transport, but thank you though.'

'Are you sure?'

'Just take her home.' So, they did just that.

Chapter 15

When they arrived home the first thing the father said was, 'I think the house needs a few changes, one sec.'

So he grabbed a screwdriver from a downstairs drawer and went upstairs, he had a plan, he knew what he was going to do, Kat was intrigued, what could he possibly want a screwdriver for? So she followed him upstairs to find out.

He went straight up to her room, sat down on the floor and started to unscrew the door off its hinges, he was no DIY man, but he could've been.

'WHAT THE ACTUAL FUCK DO YOU THINK YOU'RE DOING?' Kat screamed.

'Privacy should be earned not given,' the father stated. He continued unscrewing. He looked determined.

'This is not fair.'

'No, I'll tell you what isn't fair, hearing and seeing all about your daughter's depression from some doctor, who doesn't even know her.'

'So, your response to my depression is punishment?'

'No, don't phrase it like that.'

'Oh, I'm sorry, let me rephrase then, so your response for my depression is punishment and I'm guessing cocaine?'

'Oh, yes, thank you that reminds me to ask you, how dare you tell that boy about our private family time?'

'At least he's not the cops.'

'How dare you…'

'Just so you know if I could, right now, I would go into my room and slam the door shut to avoid you.'

'Well, you can't, I'm here so ha.'

She started crying 'I'm not a young child!'

'Then stop acting like one!'

'Yes, because all kids cut themselves!'

'No, maybe not, but they would lie. It's the lying…'

'It's not exactly the easiest thing to talk about, can't you understand that?'

He then finished, the door was off its hinges, so he went down the stairs to relax and watch television in the Living Room, his task was done, he took the Bedroom door downstairs with him. Before he left the last thing he said was, 'And you're going to school tomorrow by the way.'

Kat was just in shock, she was more than angry, she was just done, so she went into her room and without even thinking, went to slam the door that wasn't there, then sat down and played some music off her laptop. It was quite sad music, to match her mood. There was just a big gaping hole where the door should've been, a hole, hey wait, wasn't she just a hole? For other people's pleasure? She cried, oh boy did she cry.

The main reason he did it was to stop her from cutting, but he was downstairs, she was alone, she could do it now privately. So she got her knife, funny how something that was supposed to stop her from cutting, just made her do it more,

OK funny is the wrong word…Self-harm is by no means funny…

She had now successfully added to the mess that was her wrist, she went hard. Oh boy, did she go hard…

She had such a build-up of homework now that she couldn't even think about it, but even if she did, it's not like she cared. Instead of homework she put on a film, it was easier that way, she watched the film in its entirety, then put on another one and then she texted Dominic.

She said, *My dad fucked up.*

He replied basically in seconds with a *No, I fucked up.* Was he going to text her anyway? Why was he so quick? But Kat didn't wonder why.

She was now no longer watching the film, her focus was on her phone instead, her next message that she sent was *How? Explain?*

Again, he replied instantly, *You deserve an explanation in person, no you deserve more than me, can I come over?*

You're scaring me.

Sorry.

I doubt you'll be allowed to come over, but if it's important, come.

OK, see you in about half an hour.

Her anger had now been replaced with pure worry, what was going on? Something had clearly happened, but what? She didn't even inform her parents he was coming over, she would and could sneak him in.

She then thought it was wise to send him a text saying, *When you get here just text me, don't ring the doorbell, I'll sneak you in.*

It may have taken him longer than seconds to reply, but he still replied fairly quickly, I would say in a handful of minutes rather than seconds, but he said, *Today is really not the day for that kind of tomfoolery but fine, OK.*

She very softly chuckled at his message and then started nervously cleaning her room. A guest was coming! She had to clean! She just wiped various surfaces, if you could even call that cleaning, I don't think you could call wiping random surfaces cleaning.

It was more of a nervous tick. She couldn't just sit there relaxing on her laptop, it was quite clear Dominic was coming over because of something serious, but what? What could it be? Was it to break-up with her? Well, she was useless…Well, she saw herself as useless…She convinced herself it was so he could break-up with her. She was gross. She was nasty. She was dirty.

After a while, she then received a text, she didn't even need to check and see who it was from, she looked at her clock, it had been about half an hour since his message with a time stamp on it and given how now no one else texted her apart from him, she assumed it was her boyfriend announcing his appearance.

So, she went down the stairs, to the door, let him in and took him up to her room. She expected for him to give her a kiss hello, but he didn't, he just sat down on her bed, it was obvious he had been crying, but why?

He started crying, again and said, 'Just know that whatever may or may not happen, I'm in love with you.'

'That's very sweet, but once again you're scaring me, so stop it…'

She went to go sit down next to him on the bed, but didn't look at him, couldn't look at him, she was too nervous. He was still silent but he tried to grab her hand, but she didn't let him, she knew this, whatever it was, was going to be bad…

'No,' she moved her hand away from his. 'Once again, I say you're scaring me, so why don't you just tell me and hold me after.'

'After? You won't want me to touch you after.'

'Why don't you let me decide that for myself?'

It shouldn't have been possible for his tears to get stronger, but they did, his face was so wet, 'I'm so sorry.'

'If you're not going to tell me, then you can leave.' It was quite clear she was getting sick of being left in the dark.

'No, no, I've travelled all the way here,' he breathed in and out, 'the very least I can do is tell you what I did…'

'OK, I'm all ears.'

'I…'

'Yes, you what?'

'Can't even say it, get me pen and paper.'

So Kat did just that, she gave him a pen and some paper, put it on his lap and he instantly wrote one word and one word only.

CHEATED.

Was the one word he wrote.

'At what? What game were we playing?'

'The game of life.'

Kat started crying, 'Oh, fuck.'

'She wanted to sleep with me, but after the kissing, I stopped it.'

'Kissing? Oh cheers.' Oh, how she wanted her knife. 'HAVEN'T I BEEN THROUGH ENOUGH SHIT?' she shouted.

'I'm more than sorry.'

'You know what. So am I, please leave now, get out, right now, I don't even care if my parents hear you.' Hmm, was she thinking about the song *Leave (Get Out)* by JOJO by any chance?

'If that's what you want, I'm gone, but will you be OK?'

'My answer to that is unknown.'

'If you're hurting, please text me.'

'Ha, on your bike.'

He just kept his eyes on the floor and left. That was that. He left and was gone. Good riddance. Let the door hit you on the way out.

He was crying, she was crying. Aw, they were so similar! But no…They weren't…He fucked up and she was fucked over. No, she was just fucked and not in the good sense of the word. She had been raped physically, but this was something else…

It was mental, mental as in crazy, but also mental as in her head. A mental rape? It wasn't fair, why was everything so colossally shit in her life? Things could get bad in your life, that was normal, but this was colossally shit. She had actually found someone who had actually helped her, who had some of the same problems as her, but now he had hurt her the most, she couldn't stop thinking she didn't deserve help. She deserved pain and that's just what she had been given.

She couldn't even text the one she usually texted when she had a problem because he was the problem.

She felt and was, completely alone.

She tried to clean up her eyes and herself, she brushed her tears away and went downstairs for a cigarette. When she got down there, she could see her door and her tobacco, which had been left out, she was just grateful her door hadn't been burned…Yet…She couldn't be sure he wouldn't burn it…

But she grabbed her tobacco, went to go sit down and roll.

'Is that perfect timing? Or is that perfect timing?' her mother said.

'I wouldn't say it's perfect timing, but it's timing.' She was done rolling, so she stuck her cigarette in her mouth and lit it.

'No because there's food cooking in the oven.'

Kat ignored her mother, she was too busy thinking about the decision she had just made, the food that was in the oven would be her last supper, how biblical!

Now, she had to think about how he was going to do it, she wanted to and felt she deserved to die, drugs were too easy a way to do it and didn't even work, so she had to think of something else. Something that would work…It had to work…

She then came up with something, an idea, a most evil, naughty idea, it was OK that her door was gone and downstairs, she only needed a window…Her decision was that she would jump, jump out of her window, the window would give height, she needed the height…

The thought actually made her smile. Sleeping forever…Hmm, good idea, different to other attempts, but ok…Good luck, I guess…But first a last supper with her parents, then the end, beautiful friend the end (if you don't understand the band The Doors reference, you know, the song The End from Apocalypse Now, I give up…)

Her mother checked the oven. 'It's done!' she shouted, so she took the food out of the oven, put the tray on the table and got out the various utensils one needed for a meal, like plates and cutlery. The rest of the family joined her at the table, everyone sat down, but it was the father who dished up the food onto the plates and then they all started eating.

Very early on in the meal Kat unusually decided to speak, what was even more unusual was what she said, she put her fork down and said, 'I love you guys,' to her parents.

'Aw, we love you too. Are you OK? Where's that come from? You're not normally soppy...' It was the father who answered.

'Just here,' she pointed to her heart.

'That's incredibly sweet,' the mother said.

Kat didn't have any more to say, so she said nothing and they all just ate their food in silence. It didn't take them too long to finish their food, so Kat cleared away their plates and they all went to the Living Room to have a cigarette. Kat savoured each drag because she hoped it would be her last cigarette, ever.

Oh, was she hoping to give up smoking? It is a terrible habit...Yes, but not through nicotine patches...

She finished her cigarette or blem, OK, yes, it's called blem, I call it a blem, oh, I'm just going for a cheeky blem. I use London slang because this story and I are from London, bite me. Saying cigarette each time was driving me nuts, it was stressing me out, hey wait, I think I need a blem to calm down...

But she finished her BLEM and went upstairs to her room...

Chapter 16

When she walked up the stairs to her room, she couldn't even shut the door, I'm sorry but what door? So she just sat on the floor instead, it was where she felt she belonged, after all, no she felt she belonged on the ground in the garden...She had a plan. A devious plan. Almost immediately after sitting down, she started crying, no she didn't really sit, that implies there was control, it was more like she collapsed. She then pulled out her phone to text, you guessed it, Dominic, her message was short and to the point.

All she said, all she felt she needed to say was *so long and goodnight?* If I got to choose my last words, I would also pick *My Chemical Romance* lyrics...It must be said...

Why, of all times, was he busy now and not replying? Silly boy...

So she stood up and put her phone in her pocket, for no real reason, it was just something she did without thinking about it, it was just where she usually put it, but soon it wouldn't matter, it would be smashed up, along with her...She then wandered over to her window, this was it for her, this was truly it. She opened her window and looked down, it was all she could do, she took a long exhale, well, she wouldn't need the oxygen that was in her lungs soon anyway...

She turned away from the window so she was now facing her room, she stared for quite a while, she had given up trying to control her tears, OK, she now felt ready, well, as ready as she would ever feel...

So, she leaned back, it wasn't exactly a graceful way to go, the window wasn't big enough for her to just fall through, so she had to fold herself. Ha, stylish! But folding herself in order to fit through she did, she didn't even have to think about it, she just did it.

Her last thought before jumping, no, it was more falling, jumping implies she was putting a degree of energy into it, which she wasn't. But her last thought was about how shit her life had turned out, so she must deserve this. She leaned and she leaned until that was it, she was gone.

Not that it matters, but it was then that Dominic decided to reply, he said, *So long and goodnight. Cheers, thanks for scaring me.*

In another ten minutes he said, *OK, you're really starting to scare me now.*

In another ten minutes, he said, *Reply!*

And finally, in another ten minutes, he said, *On my way.*

All in all, it was about an hour after she fell that he finally arrived at her house. When he left his house, he was crying in panic, but before he even properly arrived at her house, he was full frontal weeping. He arrived in perfect timing because there was an ambulance parked outside her house, on the road.

As he was walking up her road, he could see everything up ahead, he wished he didn't but he did. On a bed she was being wheeled out of the house, all he could think was about how pretty she was, he wondered why he fucked up. But he just couldn't come up with an answer…He just couldn't do anything…

They then put her in the ambulance, both her parents were crying, but upon seeing Dominic standing outside, the father said, 'Glad to see Mr Know-It-All is here.'

'Now is really not the time to make digs at me.' Given how you were the main cause of this, I think it is…

It was the mother who answered, 'He's right.' She put her arms around the father, 'We've got bigger things to handle right now.'

Dominic nodded a thank you to the mother and went to get in the ambulance. 'And where do you think you're going?' the father asked.

'Oh, I'm just going out, what about you?'

'Where?'

But Dominic's answer was just getting into the ambulance, kneeling by her side and saying, 'We've got to stop meeting like this.'

She was connected to a machine that beeped with her heartbeat; it was such a pleasure for him to hear.

'If you ever try anything like this again, I swear down, I'll kill you myself.' He made himself laugh at that.

She was just so still, unnaturally so. If it weren't for the heart monitor, you'd think she was dead, if she was dead, that would be it for him. He couldn't live without her. He felt responsible, how could he not?

He then, just held her, then the ambulance sped off, a thought then entered Dominic's head, to phrase it nicely without profanity, he was grateful the parents weren't in the ambulance. Dominic wasn't even remotely bothered about how long it took to get to the hospital; he was too focused on Kat and her breathing.

He knew she couldn't hear him which made it easier for him to talk to her, to be honest... 'Sorry is not a big enough word to describe what I feel.' Tears started falling onto his arms, but he still held on to her. 'I'm a disgusting cheater of a person, we shouldn't be together, you deserve better. I just feel worthless, so I was shocked someone else wanted me in THAT way. It was more than stupid; I love you and I'm sorry.'

When they arrived at the hospital she was very quickly taken from the ambulance and was carried into an operating theatre, Dominic just went and waited outside. The parents joined him minutes after, they were led by a Nurse.

Who knows how long silence ensued for, but it was until Kat was ready to be taken to her room, Doctor Sharma spoke to them before she was taken, 'That went very well, I'm expecting a full recovery, she should wake up in a few hours, but her left arm and left leg are broken and she's lost a lot of blood.'

Not that he had really stopped, but once again Dominic was crying, not happy tears but happier tears. 'So, she's going to be OK?'

'I'm hoping so, yes, but still too early to be definitely sure...'

So, he and the parents followed her to her room, still silent, when they got to her room, oh how Dominic wanted to get in bed with her and hold her. But he thought, best not. So he pulled up a chair and held one of her hands while he sat by her side, the parents did the same, but on her other side.

It could've been hours or it could've been minutes before she woke up, but wake up she did, it wasn't exactly a peaceful awakening, but she was awake. The first thing she noticed was the fact she was in a hospital bed 'oh fuck,' was all she said.

She then looked around her and saw Dominic was there, she didn't smile lovingly at him, oh no, she just grimaced.

'No, not oh fuck, you just need some help, for example the therapy the doctor prescribed,' the father said.

'Well, I think my door needs therapy more than me,' it was then that she started crying. 'YOU TOOK HIM AWAY FROM HIS HOME.'

'Now is really not the time to talk about something so trivial as a door,' was the father's, quite frankly, weak defence.

'OK, fine then I guess it's good I'm pissed at all of you! Why not invite Ben to the party while you're at it?'

'Not funny,' the father said.

'Wasn't trying to be,' she crossed her arms, to say she was pissed off was putting it lightly, livid is a better descriptor.

'I'm just going to pretend you didn't say that...But can we do anything to help at all?' the father asked.

'Well, actually yes,' she started laughing. 'Can you sort me out? I'm desperate for a line.' Dominic also started laughing at that.

'OK, remember, this is hard on all of us...But l think it's time for us to leave if you're going to be like that.' So, her parents got up to leave.

'Don't let the door hit you on the way out,' she said, through laughter, Dominic also continued laughing. 'Or do, I don't care.'

Kat's laughter then subsided.

'Oh, that's good, I'm glad I amuse you,' she stated to Dominic.

'Don't be like that, I love you.'

Her arms were still crossed, 'Well, you have a funny way of showing it.'

'I know I fucked up.'

'That's putting it lightly, as a result of you telling me, I attempted suicide again, I didn't even do that after I was anally raped.'

'I know, I'm worse than a rapist, I certainly feel like it.'

'No, you're not worse than a rapist, you can't say that, but what you are is a cheater who drugged me, oh and I'm now disabled like that gopher from the zoo, but hey Survival of the Fittest, am I right or am I right?'

'I think I'd rather be a rapist.'

'Well, I wouldn't.'

'So, where does that leave us?'

'I'm pretty sure we're in a hospital room?'

'Maybe it's because I'm sorry, but I think I actually found that vaguely amusing…'

'Here all-night folks, I even tried to kill myself and I'm still here!'

'No, it was definitely that comment, all traces of humour are now gone.'

'Well, at least I amuse myself…'

'No, but can we be serious for a minute?' Dominic asked.

'Yes, of course.'

'I'm scared of the answer, but where does leave us?'

'I understand why you cheated, I'm fucked, I've been fucked, so together? Isn't that what you want?'

'What I want? No, this is about you, sweetie.'

'No, this is about us.'

'OK, true, but I'm sorry. I'm the reason this happened, you could've seriously hurt yourself or heaven forbid, died, I colossally fucked up…'

'OK, yes, that may have happened, but I still can't lose you…Deep down, I still love you, you're my true best friend, not Juliet…'

He moved his hand so it was stroking her face. 'And you won't lose me, we can still be friends, if you want, but let's go back to waiting a while or forever, for there to be an us…' He stared at her intently. 'Your choice, the ball is in your court.'

She started crying and held his hand, 'My choice?'

He didn't just hold her hand back, he clutched it, 'Your choice.' Choice was a big thing for her and I think he knew that…

She continued crying, he started crying, it wasn't pretty, they had both landed on the Water Works Monopoly square.

A doctor then entered her hospital room, he brought her parents in with him, I guess because they wanted to hear what the doctor had to say, as he came in, he was reading various sheets of paper about Kat.

'How do your limbs feel, you know, the broken ones?'

'Can't feel them.'

'That's good, it means the painkillers we gave you are working.'

'When can I go home?'

The doctor stopped looking at the sheets of paper and looked at Kat, with quite a sombre expression on his face, 'Because this was self-inflicted, I think we want to keep you in for the night, so tomorrow? A psychologist should be coming to speak to you shortly.'

'Psychologist or therapist?'

The doctor laughed. 'Note to self, she's smart, but a therapist.'

Kat glared at the doctor. 'Note to self, my doctor, who's meant to be looking after me, is in fact, a liar…'

'Last question, we need to know but how is the medication we're giving you on the whole making you feel?'

'Medication? What medication? Don't you need my consent?'

'Yes, we do, don't you want painkillers?'

'Painkillers? That's it? You stressed me out there…'

'No, there are no antidepressants, I've read your file.'

'Thank God,' Kat laughed.

'Right, I'm going to go, the therapist should be here soon.'

'Don't you mean the shrink?'

He laughed again and left and that was that. It only took minutes for the therapist to show up after the doctor left, when she arrived Kat's parents and Dominic thought it was best to give them privacy, so they also left them to it.

When they had left, it was the therapist who spoke first, 'OK, so we have privacy, that's good, I hope the doctor told you I was coming, introductions?'

'Surely, you already know my name and who I am? My name must've been written on some sheet of paper?'

'That may be, but now I'm putting a face to a name, so let me meet the actual you? OK, so, my name is Sarah, your doctor should've told you I was coming, but I'm a therapist, well, your therapist.'

Kat started laughing then asked, 'Do you prefer therapist or rapist? My name is Frodo.'

Sarah the therapist started laughing. 'Wait, no fucking way did a patient of mine save Middle Earth?' (*Lord of the Rings* jokes, you either get them or you don't…)

Kat's laughter continued, she brushed her shoulders, 'What can I say? We Bagginses are quite special…'

'OK, now let's talk seriously for a moment, was there any reason you made a rape joke back there?'

'Because I can.'

'And why is that?'

'Please leave.'

'Why?'

'I'm not getting all personal with someone I just met.'

'Does that mean you have been raped?'

But Kat didn't answer, she just stared at the floor, so the therapist left, as soon as she left, Dominic entered the room and sat where he sat earlier.

'That was a very short session, does that mean she's really good?'

Kat exhaled deeply, 'If me asking her to leave is progress, then yes.'

Dominic cackled, 'You know what, I don't think it is, but whatever floats your boat.'

'Shit, my boat has sunk.'

'No, it hasn't. You attempted to sink it, but I guess even you don't know how strong it is…'

Kat started crying at that 'why did you have to fuck up? I want to kiss you.'

'Shh, no we're friends.'

'Don't worry, I'm not, but why?'

'You know this, I'm fucked.'

Kat thought it was best to leave that conversation there, so they just talked about normal shit, her parents didn't even come back in, they just sat outside. For hours, they talked, about random shit, right up until Kat started to feel tired and yawned. 'If you're tired, go to sleep, I'm not going anywhere,' Dominic said, so Kat closed her eyes and fell asleep.

Kat's dreams weren't exactly peaceful, well, her life wasn't exactly peaceful…But when she woke up, she didn't remember them.

Chapter 17

It was fairly early when she woke up, but not ridiculously early, Dominic told the truth, he slept on the chair that was right by her bed, in reaching distance, in fact he was still asleep now, so Kat only gave him what she thought he needed, a wet willy.

'What the actual fuck? No, why? Get off me, leave me alone…' he said, turned and immediately fell back asleep.

So Kat did it again, no she didn't wet his willy, you dirty cow, she gave him a wet willy. Dominic didn't even say anything, he just stood up and saluted, lord only knows what he was saluting to, but he stood to attention.

'Morning blem?' she asked.

After fully realising her question, he stood up to attention and after his brain had fully woken up, like a droid from *Star Wars* he said, 'Roger, Roger.' Yes, his brain was fully awake and yes, he mimicked a droid from *Star Wars*, purposefully, I guess he was just strange, but you knew that already, didn't you?

'Bless,' Kat said, 'help me up?' So, they haphazardly put her in her wheelchair because her leg was broken she had a wheelchair, unconnected her from the machine that she was connected to and left the room. Dominic wheeled her. Her parents were sitting outside, still asleep, it was quite early, but luckily Kat knew where her mum kept her smokes, in her bag. So, Kat went into her bag, pulled the box out and took one and the lighter out of the box.

'Let us go!' Dominic said.

'Charge!' Kat pointed in the direction of the exit, so that was what Dominic did, he charged with her in her chair to the exit.

So, they went outside.

'I thought smokes came after breakfast?' Dominic said after she lit the blemski (I'm just fucking with you, don't worry, it's just called blem) and took a drag.

'I'm poorly, I do what I want.'

'Poorly? Oh, I'm sorry do you need to stay another night in hospital?'

Her response was glaring at him.

'No, don't worry sugar tits, we are out of here,' he shouted the last word, 'TODAY.'

'Sugar tits? I'll have you know my tits are actually on the more savoury side...You should really know, you've seen them...'

He started fake hitting his head on the wall behind him. 'Ugh, I know I've seen them, can we stop talking about your tits please?'

'OK, fine, but you started it,' Kat said quietly, but purposefully loud enough for him to hear, then she laughed.

She continued with her blem, finished it and then it was time to go back inside the hospital, when they got back to her parents, they were awake. Maybe Kat inadvertently woke them up by taking a smoke?

So Kat decided to speak to them, 'Sleep well?'

It was her mother who answered, 'To be honest, not really, but what about you?'

'Let me put it this way I'm ready for my own bed.'

'Hmm, I'm sorry, but with your broken leg, it may be a while before we can get you up the stairs to your bed…'

'Fuck. Didn't think.'

'While we're on the subject of things that are messed up, you need a new phone, you may have survived the fall, but your phone didn't.'

'Again, I say fuck.'

'Aw, bless, I hate to be the bearer of bad news, but yeah…'

'God dammit!'

'Actually, speaking of phones, Dominic I think I should have your number, but we've got to stop meeting like this.'

Dominic laughed, went over to her and they exchanged numbers.

Kat's response was, 'Cheers, Mum, don't you want my number?'

'You're number?' She laughed. 'But I know it? It's 999?'

Dominic just started laughing at that. 'Aha, good one.' He then moved his fist towards her for her to hit it, he was expecting her to fist-bump him, but she didn't know what that meant so she just stared in bewilderment.

He put his fist down.

So Kat's parents joined Kat and Dominic in her room.

'Would you like to get back into bed?' Dominic asked Kat, good lad for not just automatically assuming and doing it.

'No thanks, I'm up now.'

So, he left her in the wheelchair and collapsed on the bed himself. 'Thank God, I for one am pooped. Night!'

'OK, night!'

He replied, but fuck knows what he said, his face was too buried into pillows, I think he knew he wasn't audible because he stuck up a thumbs-up to her.

Luckily, she didn't have to wait too long with parents until a Nurse came in with Kat's breakfast, she ignored everything else in the room and just went over to a now asleep Dominic, assuming it was Kat.

'Aw, so sweet! She's asleep!' she said to herself.

'Um, no, she isn't?' Kat said. 'But just you wait until I tell him you thought he was a girl!' She started laughing. 'Hey, Dominic!' She said rather loudly, in the hopes to wake him up, it worked. Wake up, he did…

Aw. He was dreaming. He said, 'Microsoft Word? More like Microsoft turd.'

'What on Earth do you dream about?' Kat asked whilst (I really want to say she chuckled darkly because of Charlieissocoollike on YouTube, but I won't) laughing (yes much better) and looked at him.

'Good morning, Vietnam.'

'You're more than strange when you wake up.'

'Hey, I was asleep.'

'I'm aware, madam.'

'Madam?'

'See that Nurse?' Kat couldn't stop herself from laughing now. 'Right there? She thought you were a girl.'

The Nurse just put the tray of food on the side, walked towards the door, said, 'I just didn't look properly,' and left.

Kat then poured her focus onto the food, she was hungry, the others must've been hungry too, but she wasn't bothered, she just poured her breakfast into her mouth. The same doctor from the day before then entered the room as she was eating.

'Do you feel ready to leave?' was all he said.

'No, yesterday I was ready, now I'm just chomping at the bit to get the fuck out of here and go home.'

'Oh God, well, OK, you may leave.' He moved his arm down from high to low as if he was starting a race.

'Really?' She started crying.

The doctor just put his head down so he was facing her, moved it closer to hers and said, 'Really, really.'

She outstretched her arms in order to hug him, she was so grateful. He walked over, bent down and hugged her back.

'Take whatever time you need to gather your things, your parents have told me you're meant to be starting therapy this week, so please go, for me?'

'I'm on it, doc! Don't you worry, she's going, I'll make sure of it…' Dominic decided to speak, but it was still from the bed.

'If I say I trust you, it's a lie because the fact that you're laying comfortably in bed, doesn't exactly make you seem trustworthy…'

So, he stood up and got out of bed. 'How about now?'

The doctor laughed. 'Better, I guess.'

'So, can we definitely go?' the father asked the doctor.

'Yes, go, be gone!'

'Can I please take that lift home, today?' Dominic asked, probably wise after last time saying no and fucking up…

'Yes, of course, you can,' the mother said, Dominic thought it was best to avoid public transport for a while…

'Kat, we brought you some clothes from home, here you go.' She took them gratefully from her mother. If she was leaving, she didn't want to keep wearing hospital clothes and her other clothes were all messed up from the fall.

'Boys, please leave, to get dressed I need to strip.'

So, her father and Dominic left in silence, while the mother helped her get dressed. It was done quick enough, Kat was now ready to leave, she wheeled herself out of the room and as she went away from it, she stuck her middle finger up at the room. She had left the room; it was now no longer hers. Dominic started wheeling her. 'Is it OK if I jump in your car with you?' he whispered to her.

'Well, given last time you said no and you fucked up, I'm going to say yes, but not because I like you or heaven forbid like spending time with you…'

He laughed. 'Charming.'

'No, it's fine, come on in.'

'If you're sure…?'

'I wouldn't have said yes if I wasn't sure.'

Oh, how he wanted to kiss her and hold her, she was alive with all her marbles intact, he hadn't completely lost her either, she had got off luckily, which meant he had got off luckily…She only had a few broken bones which in time would heal…

On the way out, the parents filled in some paperwork, a receptionist asked if they wanted an ambulance to take her home because she was in a wheelchair, they thought it was wise to say yes. So, they waited by the exit, it didn't take a ridiculously long amount of time for the ambulance to show up and then it was time to leave.

Dominic went with the dad, so he could drop him off back home, so Kat went and took the ambulance with her mum because they would most likely get home before the dad, so she would let them in.

'See you at school tomorrow,' he said.

'Will you?' Kat started laughing. 'I'm quite liking these hospital trips...'

'Just shut the fuck up.'

Was the last thing he said to her before they went their separate ways. She got in the ambulance and he got in the car. The drive in the ambulance wasn't too long, when they reached their destination, the mother opened the door and the paramedics carried Kat downstairs because the mother asked them to. Downstairs there was food, sofas to sleep on, a TV and a toilet, everything a young disabled girl needed. When Kat was safely down there, it was time for the paramedics to leave, so they did and shut the front door behind them.

'Christ only knows how we'll get you to school tomorrow, maybe your dad will drive you?' the mother said because she couldn't drive.

'Or I could just not go?'

'I'm not even going to answer that...'

'But I nearly died, I need more time.' She rolled herself a blem and lit it. Now, slow death by smokes it had to be.

But the mother didn't reply to that, so, that was the conversation over, so, Kat, still in her wheelchair, stuck the TV on, watched it and waited for the father to return. When he arrived, the mother made him a cup of tea, he took control of the remote and he asked his daughter how she was.

'But I'm disabled,' she said as if trying to mimic the IT Crowd, it didn't work, her parents hadn't even seen it...

'Don't say that, that's not fair, this whole situation has been hard on all of us.'

'You're yet to ask me why I did it.'

He tore his gaze away from the TV and onto Kat, then he asked, 'OK, fine, why did you do it? Was there a specific reason?'

Kat was now conflicted, should she be honest? He'll only wish he'd dropped Dominic in a sceptic tank and not at home, so no, maybe it was best not to…

'I just felt trapped, like I couldn't escape,' that's a very specifically vague answer, impressive, good thinking, I commend you. A lie, but a good lie.

'Why didn't you speak to us?'

'Do I really need to say it again?' She shouted the last word, 'TRAPPED.'

'Do you feel better?'

'I really want to say yes, I'm peachy, but let's be real, now my body is now just as fucked up as my mind.'

The father didn't verbally reply to that, he just started crying.

'I'm sorry, I didn't mean to make you cry, the truth is a bitch.'

Saying that really did it, he wasn't just crying anymore, no, he started wailing.

The rest of the day was just spent watching TV; for dinner, they even got a takeaway and ate it in front of the TV, they were addicted.

When it got to midnight the father said, 'It's kind of perfect really, if I'm taking you to school tomorrow, so we both need our sleep, so you can sleep uninterrupted down here because I'm going up to bed, all good!'

'Hmm, I wouldn't say that's perfect, I think your definition of perfection varies greatly from mine...' Kat said.

Kat's mother then helped to lift her onto the sofa and got a duvet out for her.

'Goodnight, darling!' the mother said and she went up the stairs.

'Goodnight, darling!' the father said and did the same and turned the lights out.

Kat was now alone, so she said, 'Night,' to nothing and went to sleep, she didn't even have a phone anymore, so no alarm, not that she wanted them to, but she knew, in the morning, her parents would wake her up. So she went to sleep, but she still wished it was forever…

Chapter 18

The next morning, her mother came downstairs first to wake Kat up and get her dressed, when Kat was all ready and in her chair, it was breakfast time! So, her mother made her daughter a bowl of cereal and turned her work computer on.

'Thank you,' Kat said and just started eating.

The mother said nothing and just heated up three mugs of coffee in the microwave, one for each of them. Before Kat was even finished eating, her father came down the stairs, he was very chipper that morning, almost too chipper...No wrong word, definitely too chipper...

'And how is my darling daughter this morning?' He sat at the table and started rolling himself a cigarette.

'Jeez, are you sure you can drive? Oh, it's fine, I just won't go to school...You're very energetic this morning and no breakfast or did you have cocaine for breakfast, yikes?' Kat made herself really laugh at that because cocaine for breakfast, yikes are lyrics by Frank Ocean in the song Novacane. Listen to it. You're welcome.

'Oh God, I think you must have hit your head, your sense of humour has gotten worse.' He didn't know the song...

'Too soon,' but the very mention of her humour reminded her of Dominic...In order to text him, like usual, she needed, a phone! So she asked, 'Can I please borrow one of your old phones for my day at school?'

'Good memory! Because your phone is broken...The doctor said you hit your head quite hard, so your memory may be damaged...' The mother exclaimed, 'but yes, of course, you can.'

'What can I say? I'm a screenager through and through...' Screenager is from an article she did in English...

But the mother didn't reply, she just went upstairs to find a phone, she came back downstairs quite quickly. 'You'll need to charge it, but you can do that at school, can't you?'

'You're lucky I know your numbers off by heart, um what about SIM card?'

'Fuck, OK, at end of school wait for your father at reception?'

Kat put the phone on the table, looked at her father, 'Please don't be late.' Then she had a cigarette. 'How am I even going to get to all my lessons? Stairs are involved for some of them?'

'Shit, call the school, we haven't fucking told them, they need to know she's in a chair!' The mother said to the father and visibly started panicking.

The father grabbed his phone and called the school.

'Hi, so this is Kat Campbell's dad, she took a little tumble and is now in a wheelchair, can she come in?'

He looked pensive as he was listening. 'No, that's perfect, thank you, OK bye.' He put his phone down and smiled.

'No, it's all OK, they have other disabled kids there, so it may take them the rest of the week to get everything settled, like by moving lessons that are upstairs to somewhere downstairs, but after that, it should be normal.'

'Oh, joy!' Kat said, very sadly.

'Yes! That's the right reaction! Oh, joy indeed! But can I get a little more excitement please?' the father said and lifted up his arms to signal he wanted a lot of excitement.

'Oh, joy,' Kat whispered.

'Get in the car, we'll work on your optimism on the way.' So, he stood up and started his journey towards the stairs so he could go up them, he hadn't noticed or even thought about his daughter, so he went up them.

'Let's see how long it takes him to notice I've not walked up with him,' the wheelchair-bound Kat said, the mother just put her head in her hands.

The father was about to open the front door when he realised, he left the keys in the door and ran downstairs.

'I'm so sorry!' he exclaimed.

'No, no, go without me, I don't mind!'

Then the mother and the father picked Kat up, took her to the stairs and carried her up.

'I have never been so happy that you're not fat,' the mother said.

'That might just be the weirdest compliment I've ever received, so thank you!'

It didn't take them long to climb the stairs, the father went outside, unlocked the car doors and together both the mother and father lifted Kat into a passenger seat in the car.

The father went to go put the wheelchair in the boot.

'Actually, can you come with us? We might need you when we get there.'

'Yes, of course!' The mother exclaimed, 'Road trip!' She locked the front door to the house and got in the car.

'Can't we go somewhere more interesting on our road trip or at least somewhere not so shit...?' Kat asked.

'Somewhere more interesting than the fountain of knowledge that is school? Doesn't exist, sorry,' the father answered, laughed and started driving. The journey wasn't too long, it was too early for traffic and so they got there quick enough. When they arrived, the parents put Kat in her wheelchair.

'See you later!' the mother said and waved.

'Yes, but please be on time,' Kat pleaded, 'if you can get me to school on time, you can take me away on time.'

'Ugh, yes OK, stop harping on about times,' the father said.

Kat's reply was just a grimace.

She was then ready for school, well, as ready as she would ever be, so she wheeled herself away from her parents and into school, the other students who walked past her were still half asleep, so she didn't have to talk. Luckily, her form was on the bottom floor, so when it was time, she was able to wheel herself in there.

Upon looking at her, her form tutor said, 'My God, what happened to you? Is it forever? Or will you get better? Are you OK?'

Kat, once again, copied the IT Crowd, laughed and said, 'I'm disabled.'

'Yes, I can see that. But how?'

'I fell,' because saying she jumped was too much for her and she was sure he didn't want to hear that...

'You poor thing.'

'Don't worry, it shouldn't be permanent, my leg just needs to heal up.'

'Thank God.'

'You may very well, thank God, but I thank the doctors.'

'Well, yes...Them too...'

Her morning drifted by slowly, then it got to break. When it got to break, she was excited until she realised, she couldn't go to the top of the Science Block for a cheeky blem.

She put her head in her hands and groaned, so she went to the Dining Hall and got some food, she had to get her oral pleasure from somewhere, hashtag Freud. If it wasn't through smoking, it had to be through food. So she bought some cheese on toast and moved her chair towards a table.

Dominic saw her, came over to her and sat down opposite her, 'Why are you here and not smoking?'

'It's currently not a suitable activity for disabled people,' she laughed, aw, it was good to see they were slowly attempting to get back to normal, laughing definitely helped.

After break she had to climb some stairs to get to her next lesson and as she hadn't been told of any location changes yet she basically had no lesson at all, which was great! Until she got bored quickly because no mobile, so she ended up reading a textbook anyway, to pass the time.

Her next lesson, she could get to, so she went. When it got to lunch, she typically sat with Dominic. They just talked normal chit-chat, nothing special. The rest of the day was fairly average, until it was over, so she went to reception as previously discussed and waited for her parents...

She kept waiting for her parents...She even wished Dominic was there, that's how bored she was there, their relationship may have been rocky at that moment in time, but he was still someone to talk to. After what felt like and was an hour her parents finally arrived.

'So sorry, we're late, work has been truly crazy today,' was the mother's apology, the father said nothing.

'Didn't I specifically ask you to be on time?'

'It's not like we didn't want to be.'

'Ugh, whatever, can we go please?'

'Yes, of course.'

So, Kat started to wheel herself out of the reception, it was quite commendable really, she only asked for help with her wheelchair if she really needed it, otherwise she was determined and wanted to do everything herself.

They quickly arrived at the car and Kat said, 'Please, I'm dying for a Blem, can I have one, then we go?'

'OK, but be quick,' the mother said.

'I'll be quicker if I have one of yours and don't have to roll?' Ha, Kat, next time just ask, they're more expensive for a reason. You're paying for the easiness.

The mother grumbled and passed Kat one of her cigarettes and joined her daughter in sticking one in her mouth.

'Oh, by the way, we got you a SIM card.'

'Aw, good memory, thank you!'

Then the father interrupted, 'That's fine, I'll just be the driver, I know my place, leave me out of your smoke circle…'

'OK, thank you, we will,' Kat said, laughed and lit her cigarette.

The mother joined her, 'What a kind driver…'

When they were done, just like in the morning they put Kat in the car and put her wheelchair in the boot. The parents then got in the car.

'Ready?' the father asked generally.

'I don't know, am I ready? I mean really?' Kat asked, but the father just ignored her and started driving.

The journey home was average, it wasn't particularly slow, it wasn't particularly quick, but it was safe, much to Kat's dismay. If she thought life was shit enough to commit suicide before getting disabled, well, now she was disabled she was just on a whole other level of wanting to die. It was awful.

When they arrived at home, the parents carried Kat down the stairs, when she was down there, she actually decided to do some homework on the little tray on her wheelchair. How productive! After a while, her homework was done, completed, finished. Maybe she should've got disabled much earlier if it meant she actually did her homework, you know at home? But when it was done, she decided to watch TV, well, what else was she going to do? Read? Don't be ridiculous! How about no…

After about another half hour the parents then stopped working, the father came to the Living Room to watch TV, whereas the mother put some food in the oven from the freezer for dinner. Gordon Ramsey would be proud…

'Oh yes, phone?' she asked when the food was in the oven and she sat down.

'Actually, no thanks, I'm OK, it may be a pain in the ass me not having one, but I think it'll be good for me.'

'Your choice, I guess. Does that mean you'll always be waiting for us at the reception?'

'Even if I had a phone, that's where I'd be.'

'Jeez, OK, I was just checking…'

And that concluded that conversation between Kat and her mother for now.

It only took about three-quarters of an hour for the food to get ready, again they had a TV dinner and a TV evening, interspersed with various cigarettes. When it got to eleven, so an hour earlier than the day before, the father announced, 'Fuck, you get up early, I'm knackered, goodnight, bed calls.' So, he turned the TV off, went upstairs and silently the mother joined him.

'So what? Am I just supposed to sleep in my chair? Cheers,' Kat said to nothing because no one was there, so she put the TV on and watched some crap and had a smoke.

Then Kat had a thought, a devious thought. Her mum's phone was right there, behind her, on charge and so she went over to it, to text Dominic, it was good they had exchanged numbers. She knew she shouldn't, but she could, so she did.

I love how you fuck up and you're still in control of our relationship and where we go from here, the fact that I did this to myself shows I need help, I need some control, so cheers, was what Kat sent and said.

As per Dominic replied quickly *Kat's mum?*

Yes, you twat.

Did I make a good joke? Or did I make a good joke?

No, what you made is a shit show.

A shit show? But you hung out with me at school?

Don't remind me, it's not fair that I still love you.

Well, ha, I love you more, but as a friend...For now...

She could've easily kept texting him, but decided against it, instead she deleted all the texts, between herself and Dominic so her mother wouldn't ask questions the next day and put her mother's phone back on charge. She carried on watching TV, she did sleep a bit but it wasn't the most restful sleep because you know…She was in a chair…

Chapter 19

The next day, the TV was still on, but Kat's mother woke her up, Kat swung her head and was then awake, almost peacefully but not peacefully.

'Oh shit, were you in that chair all night? I'm so sorry.'

'GOOD MOANING,' she shouted, she still wasn't quite with it.

'Come on, let's get you dressed for school and get some breakfast down you.'

Kat's morning was very similar to that of the day before, wake up, get dressed, break the fast, wash the food down with a smoke, get in the car and leave to go to school.

When they reached their destination, just like yesterday, Kat's parents got her into her wheelchair and left. Kat was ecstatic because they hadn't mentioned the therapy. Had they forgotten? Did this mean she didn't have to go? Get in!

So once again she went into school, they had shifted some of her classrooms around so she missed no lessons, although after lunch was a P.E. lesson and somehow, I don't think saying the dog ate my homework was going to help her. It was then lunchtime, so she got her food and sat opposite Dominic, before she had even fully arrived at the table, he asked her, 'Are you looking forward to starting therapy tonight?'

'Bugger. You weren't supposed to remember…'

'How could I forget?'

'Shame then that I have a previous engagement, my parents are picking me up.'

'Then it's a good thing I know that your mum's number works, I can just text her and tell them not to come.'

'You wouldn't,' she crossed her arms.

He looked down for a minute, then pulled his phone out from under the table and laughed. 'Shame I just did.'

'You fucker.'

But he just laughed at that.

In between bursts of laughter, he said, 'In all seriousness, I hope it helps you, it does me.'

'I've got plenty of people I can talk to. Why use one that costs money?'

'Other than me who've you got? Go on, I'm listening…'

She had to think for a few minutes, 'Umm, Juliet?'

'Oh really? Have you informed her about any of the more recent and serious developments in your life?'

She took a swig of her drink, said, 'No, but I'm about to,' to prove her point she left Dominic on his own and went to find Juliet.

She wasn't too far away, she was sat in the Dining Hall, with a finished tray of food in front of her and she was sat with some girls who Kat didn't really know who were in their school year. She wheeled herself up to the table.

'My God, Kat, I've missed you, how did this even happen?' She pointed at the wheelchair and gave her a big hug.

Kat returned the hug. 'Well, actually, I was meaning to, well hoping to talk to you in private. Boy, have we got a lot to talk about…'

'In private? But with Dominic?'

'No, in private, as in in private.'

'Oh, dear God, yes, I've missed you.' She stood up, didn't even clear her tray away and just sat on Kat's lap, Kat started wheeling them out of the Dining Hall.

'Where to, madam?' Kat asked. 'You're so sweet, I've missed you.'

'No, it is I who have missed you, you're now always with your boyfriend, what happened to bros before hoes?'

Kat laughed. 'But you are a hoe?'

'Just because you're now a cripple, doesn't mean I'm not afraid to use violence and knock some sense into you.'

'Duly noted.'

Together they wandered off, well wheeled off to the fields to talk, Juliet then got off of Kat's lap and sat on the grass.

'I'm fucking dying for a fag,' Kat said.

'Oh shit, I didn't even think about that, you poor sod, I'm guessing you can't get up to the roof of the Science Block?'

Kat just shook her head.

'If it's any consolation, I'm trying to cut down and maybe even give up, so we're both in the same boat, in terms of wanting one.'

'Please no more cigarette talk, I just can't.'

'Oh shit, of course, what shall we talk about?'

'Um, me?'

'Go for it.'

'So, quite a lot has occurred in my life since we last spoke. some good things, some bad things…' was how Kat started.

'It's quite obvious you've ditched Ben for a younger model.'

'Oh, Christ, this is going to take a while…'

'Well, I'm listening,' she leant back.

'Hmm, where to start…?'

'OK, so, what happened to Ben?' She started laughing. 'Did you need some younger spice in your life?'

'Not exactly…' Kat sat up straighter. 'I have two things to say to that…'

'How about I just sit here silently while you speak?'

'That may be wise.'

So, Juliet moved her hand as if locking her lips.

Juliet's lips were now locked, it was time for Kat to start, but she asked, 'Where do I even start?'

'At the beginning?'

'I think that lock of yours is broken.'

So, Juliet locked her lips again, she was ready.

'Hmm, at the beginning? Well, OK…' Kat tried to steady herself, she succeeded, so she started, 'Well, OK, my parents are quite messed up.'

Juliet nodded extremely.

'Messed up as in they're both partial to a little white powder and sharing it with me.'

'I'm sorry for speaking but how can I keep quiet? White powder?'

'Of the illegal variety…'

'Fuck and how do you feel about that?'

'I think the word fuck is a good descriptor…'

'Does it happen often?'

'Fridays and Saturdays because heaven forbid doing it on a school night.'

'Does Dominic help?'

'As much as he can, which to be honest, isn't very much, so no.'

'Are you guys together?'

'Long story, don't worry I'll save your ears.'

'OK, Ben?'

'Is out of my life for good, fucker…'

'Care to explain?'

Kat gave herself a minute to wonder whether or not to be honest.

'Come on, you can tell me? I mean it's not like he raped you?' Wrong words Juliet, WRONG WORDS.

'So, does that mean if he did rape me, I shouldn't tell you?'

Juliet started crying, I think she knew the answer, but she still asked, 'Well, did he?'

'My only experience of anal sex.'

'FUCK.'

'Aha yes, I was well and truly fucked.'

'How can you make jokes about something so serious?'

'It's a skill I have, that hasn't been lost,' she pointed to her wheelchair.

'Oh yeah, thanks for reminding me, not that I needed reminding, you're sat in it, but wheelchair? Why? How?'

Again Kat thought, the thought that came to mind was honesty was the best policy but was it in all situations? Hmm, was it? 'I'm so clumsy, I fell, oops.'

'Not going to lie, I thought you did.'

I think that response makes it obvious Kat hadn't disclosed any previous attempts to her…

'Ahaha, indeed.'

Juliet also laughed. 'I swear you're going to kill yourself one of these days.'

Kat kept on laughing but deep down wished hopefully she would indeed kill herself.

'Anyway, enough about me, what about you?'

'My life is so much more boring than yours, swear down.'

'Shut up, spill.'

'OK, so now, I'm regularly texting George, finally, it's going well, he's quite a nervous character, I'm hopeful he'll ask me out soon though. A girl can dream…'

To Kat, this was huge news, Juliet fancying George had been ongoing for months. 'That's huge! Get in my son!' To really show her excitement she punched the air.

'It's really not that exciting…'

'Do you ever hang out in person?'

'We had lunch together last week…'

'I can hear wedding bells…'

Juliet punched Kat in the shoulder.

Then the bell then rang to signify the end of lunch.

'I've missed you, come to talk to me more, but I understand why you haven't don't worry, my God, have you been through it.'

'Appreciated, I will, my phone died more than me in the fall and I'm enjoying being off the grid, but when I get a new one, I'll text you.'

'Sweet.'

That was it, that was the deep meaningful conversation over, the DMC, see, look, I'm down with the kids, I know slang, text speak, whatever you want to call it…

When Kat arrived at her form room it was normal and boring, then she remembered it was P.E. next, she even said, 'Ah fuck,' out loud.

'What's wrong Kat?' her form tutor asked.

'We've all got P.E. next.'

'Aw do you not like P.E.? It'll be home time soon enough.'

Kat was amazed by his stupidity, she pointed to herself, 'Look at me, I mean really look at me…Can I even do P.E.?'

'Oh gosh, of course, you don't have to go, you can go to the library if you want instead.'

Kat laughed. 'To the library? Up the stairs?'

'Oh gosh, I'm sorry, it's been a long day…'

'How about I just go to an empty classroom and do some work there?'

'Yes, good idea, do that.'

'Yes, sir!'

'Actually, I think this room is free, so you can stay here.'

She thought about asking if she could just go home, but she only thought about it because she knew her form tutor would say yes, to avoid therapy and to have a cigarette more than anything, but, given her physical state, she was unsure about public transport and no phone meant she couldn't exactly order a taxi. So, she was stuck at school, the fact it would upset Dominic didn't even cross her mind.

Then everyone else left the classroom and went to P.E. apart from her form tutor, who went to whichever class he had to teach next. Kat logged into the computer on the teacher's desk, all the computers in school were the same, so she could log in, anywhere. It was a shame that YouTube or anything vaguely fun was blocked, so she begrudgingly did some homework, whilst listening to music.

Finally, the bell rang to signify the end of school, but she didn't leave her form room, she didn't want to find Dominic, she didn't want to go to therapy.

Chapter 20

Unfortunately for Kat, in about twenty-three minutes Dominic barged into her form room and found her, I don't know why I said in about? Twenty-three minutes is quite specific.

'My God, I've been looking everywhere for you, I even went to reception to find out where you could be, upon hearing you had P.E. last, I assumed you wouldn't go because why would you? Thank our Father who art in heaven, you stayed in your form room.'

'God dammit.'

But she couldn't deny it was sweet he actually had to try to find her and succeeded, she felt special…

'Shall we go? I spoke to someone and ordered you an ambulance last night. I didn't even know you could do that?' He started laughing. 'What are they? Taxi cabs?'

'If they charge us a fare, I think you did it wrong.'

Kat joined in with the laughter, but then Dominic just stopped. 'The ambulance just texted me, they're on the road waiting for us.'

'Help me, I'm beyond nervous…Therapy?' She laughed. 'See I always knew I was fucked, but now it's official…'

'No, don't be nervous, I'll be right there, if it's anything like mine, it's just a pair of ears to listen to you and you love to talk, so no problem?' That brought his laughter back.

She grabbed and held onto the desk. 'You can't make me go!'

He thought his response before saying it, it made him laugh. 'You're disabled, so I think you'll find I can.'

As if to prove a point, without even logging her off or collecting her stuff, he just wheeled her out of there.

'My stuff!'

'Will still be there tomorrow, like you're going to do homework when you get home! As if! Remember I know you…'

'Touché.'

He wheeled her all the way outside.

'Hey, I'm coming, I'm coming, I can wheel myself, stahp.'

'Sorry, of course, you can, but to be fair, there was no way you were going to come on your own accord originally, so you needed the help.'

'OK fair,' Kat laughed at that.

They then walked to the school gate and left the school grounds; well, Kat didn't walk, she wheeled herself out, the ambulance was close enough to the gate for them to easily locate. So, they went over to it.

'Can I please have a cigarette before we leave? I could kill for one…I'm literally begging you…' Kat asked a Paramedic.

'Ugh, yes, but please be quick.'

Kat had started rolling before the Paramedic answered, she was good with being quick, she just needed a nicotine hit, immediately. When she was done rolling, she sparked it and inhaled deeply and exhaled deeply. She was in bliss.

Kat enjoyed her Blem in its entirety, my God, she needed it, then she said, 'Ready,' very little was said, very little needed to be said, but in minutes they were all loaded into the ambulance and ready to go.

Kat felt more than nervous, so she was silent the whole way there, Dominic wasn't blind, he could see her nervousness on her face so he held her hand.

She let him hold it, well she didn't move her hand away but said, 'Hmm, isn't hand holding romantic?'

'I have two working eyes, but if you want me to stop, I'll stop, you just look scared, my hand is just there to let you know I'm there, but I'll stop.'

He pulled his hand away.

'No, come back,' Kat said and pulled his hand back.

He laughed and allowed for his hand to be pulled back, 'Thought so.'

She just stared out the window and nervously clutched and squeezed Dominic's hand for the whole journey.

'Hey, please don't squeeze so hard. Ow!'

'Sorry! Accident!'

'No problem! Hey, how bout I get you a stress ball?'

'If you do, get me a nicely shaped one because it's going straight up your ass.'

'So, no?'

'Do whatever you want, but you can't say I didn't tell you what I'd do with it…'

'Well, I don't think my ass is particularly stressed, so I don't think it needs a stress ball, so how bout I leave it for now?'

'Your choice...'

Then they arrived at the hospital, well at therapy, so they unloaded themselves from the ambulance, thanked the Paramedics and went to the smoking area near the hospital entrance. Kat quickly had a cigarette because she felt she needed to brace herself before going inside.

It was all going swimmingly, well that was until they arrived at the entrance, Kat held onto the wall outside and said 'I'm not going in, you can't make me.'

Dominic laughed. 'But we've already established that I can and I will, so the real question is would you like me to wheel you? Or would you like to wheel yourself?'

'You bastard.'

'No, all my immediate family are still alive, thanks.'

'Fine, you can be a see you next Tuesday instead.' (Now, I thought to see you next Tuesday was a worldwide thing, but upon hearing it's not, let me explain, so see you is C U and take the first letters off next Tuesday, which gives you an N and a T. Put it all together and you magically get the word CUNT.)

'Rude.'

'No, I'm disabled and I'm Kat, who's rude?' That made her laugh, but it just made him wheel her into the hospital, she was far from happy about it.

Her laughter was quickly replaced by his laughter, he just about got the words out, 'Serves you right.'

Kat just crossed her arms and also said, 'Rude.'

His laughter continued. 'Wait a second...You're rude...I'm rude...Hey, maybe we should be together?'

'I'll bite you.'

'Aw, bless, no you can try.'

So she tried, to bite him, oh boy did she try. Her attempts were kind of sweet but pathetic, he didn't even have to lift up his hand and stop wheeling her.

When they reached the reception to walk past it, Dominic asked a receptionist, 'Where do we go for therapy?'

A receptionist quickly answered, 'Sorry, today has been a bit of a mess, we'd normally give you a room, but I don't think we can today, so you'll have to go to where the therapists are, which is to the left.' She pointed in the right direction and then said, 'Oops,' and then pointed in the left direction...

'Appreciated. Thank you,' Dominic said and wheeled a Kat who was far less than happy in the direction the receptionist had pointed out.

When they arrived, there was a door labelled THERAPISTS, so Dominic opened it and they went inside. There were only three therapists in there and many more empty desks.

'This here is Kat,' he pointed to her, 'she is supposed to start therapy, well now...Please help us, we were told to come here.'

'Ah yes, that's me,' one of the therapists stood up, she outstretched her hand and shook Kat's hand rather than Dominic's. Well, Kat may have been disabled, but she was still the patient, so it was good she shook her hand, it helped her feel like a person. Maybe it's a therapy thing, I don't know, but it was good because Kat felt like she was easily forgotten about in comparison to her able-bodied counterparts...

'Where shall we go?' the therapist asked, but Kat didn't reply. 'Oh God, can she speak?' the therapist asked Dominic.

'No, I'm mute.' Kat laughed as she said it.

'Good to hear you have a sense of humour.'

Dominic laughed. 'Oh, you have no idea…'

'There's a therapy room back there, shall we go?'

'But I can't exactly sit on the sofa like I'm supposed to…?'

'Your sense of humour is tickling me.'

'And I think that concludes our therapy session for today, bye!' Kat said and wheeled herself to the door.

Dominic stopped her and just said, 'No.'

'Why do you want to leave? I just want to talk to you?' the therapist lady said.

'Ugh, for fucks sake, fine.'

'Good luck doc, you'll need it,' Dominic said to the therapist. 'But I'll be waiting outside for you, good luck,' he said to Kat and left.

That was it.

The end.

Dominic left, so it was just Kat and the therapist remaining.

'Please proceed, let's go!' the therapist said and pointed to the therapy room, so Kat may not have wanted to, but she led the way.

When they got in there, the therapist sat down on a chair and, well, Kat sat in her chair. 'My last experience with a therapist didn't go so well, just so you know.'

'Well, I'm not them, this room here is your space, you can talk about anything you want here, in fact you don't have to talk about anything at all here, no in fact times two we don't have to have these sessions at all, it's your choice to be there. I firmly believe in patient choice, yes, a doctor sent you here, but it's your choice to stay.'

'No, I'm intrigued, I'll stay…'

'Excellent, glad to hear it, OK formal introductions time, my name is Anna.' She outstretched her hand.

'Dominic has already introduced me?'

'Does Dominic always introduce you? Does he speak for you? Shall I go get him?'

'No, Christ, my name is Kat.'

'Meow.'

'You're weird.'

'That may be,' she laughed, 'but I'm also someone you can talk to.'

'Talk to? How long you got?'

'The rest of the hour, until next week, I'm guessing that means you have a lot to say? Would you like to start?'

'Not really.'

'OK, then I'll start, is the wheelchair new? I'm guessing it is because the doctor didn't mention it, when he set this up, by this I mean us meeting, obviously…'

'Very, very new.'

'May I ask why you're in it?'

'Sure, I fell.'

'Fell? From what may I ask?'

'My bedroom window,'

'My God, what were you doing?'

Kat had to think about whether or not, to be honest for a sec. 'What was I doing? Hmm, smelling the flowers.'

'Did they smell nice?'

'No, well, it didn't fucking work,' Kat started crying at that.

'Didn't work?'

'Yes, suicide take three didn't work, but fuck me, I don't think I could've gotten much closer, do you? I mean look at me.'

'Just know, that's a huge thing you've just admitted to, I hope you know that, I wasn't expecting that today.'

'Well, I surprise even myself.'

'How do you feel about it now?'

'Pissed.'

'Angry? Why?'

'It didn't work again; I can't even do that right.'

'Well, I'm happy it didn't work because if it had, I wouldn't have got to meet you.'

'What are your first impressions of me? Do you think I'm fucked?'

'Wait, how old are you?'

Kat laughed. 'Three.'

'If you're not going to be honest with me, you're an ex-patient, it'll be on your file.'

'Ugh, OK, fine, fifteen.'

'Wow, you seem old beyond your years.'

'Perks of being fucked I guess, but it doesn't get me served alcohol in the shop.'

'Do you often try to get served?'

'No, I may be many things, but a piss head is not one of them.'

'So what do you do to relax?'

Oh God, Kat knew where this conversation was going to end up, hopefully Anna would end up being trustworthy.

'I do drugs to relax.'

'With friends?'

Oh fuck.

'And with,' oh, double fuck 'parents'.

'Parents? Goodness and how does that make you feel?'

Kat laughed again. 'High.'

'No, emotionally.'

'Like it's just another carriage on my fucked-up train. Choo Choo! All aboard!'

'Does making jokes help?'

'Not particularly, I just don't want to be seen as miserable.'

'But please be aware, you have every right to be sad, you've been through some pretty serious stuff by the sounds of it.'

'I haven't even told you the worst thing…'

'I'm listening…'

'OK, give me a minute to brace myself to say it.'

'OK, I'm right here when you're ready.'

Kat focused on her breathing, in and out, in and out.

'I think I'm ready now.'

'Then go for it.'

'My now ex-boyfriend anally raped me.'

'Fuck.'

Anna's response made Kat laugh again, God she was such a comic. 'Yes, I was, wouldn't recommend it to a friend.'

'Are you even vaguely, OK? Wait, no, I know the answer to that, the suicide attempts suggest no…Sorry, stupid question…'

'Oh, my God! Are you a therapist or something? Those powers of deduction though! Amazing, truly amazing.'

'I think we need to make you a joke chart…'

'That can be your homework then.'

'On it! Next week, same time?'

Oh, how Kat wanted to say if I must, but she knew that would only be met with another lecture about choice, so she just said, 'OK.'

'I think that concludes our first session; how did you find it?'

'Aren't you supposed to help me? You know give me therapy because you're, you know, a therapist? But I just spoke?'

'I would like to and I have to get to know you a little bit first before I can try and help you, you know, job description…'

'Me as in me? Or my case?'

'You as in you, I don't know about you, but I don't think I've spent the last hour talking to some case?'

'OK, fair.'

'See you this time next week?'

'You'd have to kill me to keep me away.'

'Judging by what we've spoken about, poor joke.'

'Maybe it wasn't a joke…'

'Take care of yourself and hopefully see you next week.' Anna gave Kat a wave to signify goodbye.

Anna made Kat laugh again, therapist or comedian? Who knows… 'Wait, was that a poor attempt at a joke?'

'Sorry, no, hate to break it to you, but I'm a therapist, not a comedian.'

'Speaking of which, I'm impressed, I can't believe I actually felt comfortable talking to you, I may not trust you yet, but it's certainly heading in that direction.'

'That means a lot.'

That was the session over, that was it, so Kat decided to leave the room and went to go and find Dominic, while Anna scribbled some notes in her notebook.

Chapter 21

Kat may have found that whole ordeal quite strange, no bizarre, but it was nice just being able to talk to someone, to talk it out perhaps? Or maybe it just felt intrusive, she couldn't decide which one it was, but she went, it was done, now she could relax and not talk. Ha maybe if she was going to meet anyone other than Dominic, she was sure he'd want an in-depth analysis of the whole ordeal.

When he saw her, he jumped up and borderline skipped over to her, no he did skip, there was nothing borderline about it.

The very first thing he said when she had wheeled herself out to him was, 'I'm proud of you for going.'

Her reply was, 'Come on, outside, let's go,' oh boy, did she feel she needed to smoke a cigarette now, to help her feel calmer…

So together, they left the hospital, Kat had even started rolling before they left the building…She was desperate…

They were outside when it was fully rolled, Kat was wheeling quite quickly, so she lit it, quickly and deeply inhaled a drag of her Blem and finally replied to Dominic, 'Let's be honest, I didn't exactly have a choice in going, did I?'

But where are his questions about it? So far Kat has asked more…

'Would you like to go get some dinner?' That question may have been from Dominic, but it doesn't count, ask her about the therapy…?

Ah, OK, was he was saving his questions for at dinner? But Kat just looked nervous and stared at the floor, she knew dinner meant talking and was she ready for that? To put it bluntly, no, hence the nervous look…

'I'm going to take your silence as a yes. Dominic, I'm starving, let's go, now!' Dominic said and laughed.

He took her in his arms, well he took her wheelchair into his arms and they went to go find a restaurant.

It didn't take them very long to find one.

'Just be aware, this is my treat to you, I'm paying, so get what you want, don't look at the price.' Aw, what a gentleman!

As fucking if Kat was going to let him pay for everything, it's not like they were going out? 'Very chivalrous,' was all she said.

So, they entered the restaurant, given the time it was very quiet, they were quickly given a table and a menu each.

'Thank you,' Dominic said to the waiter and he started to look through the menu. Kat also looked through the menu, in a matter of minutes the waiter came back with some water.

'Any drinks orders?'

'A large glass of house white please?' Kat asked.

'No problem, but can I see some ID please?'

Bugger, oh did she wish she looked older, to keep up appearances she checked all her pockets, 'Sorry, I must've left it at home.'

'Then sorry we can't serve you alcohol.'

'That's OK, I understand.'

'OK, I think I'm now ready to order!' Dominic exclaimed.

'Can we order food with you?' Kat asked the waiter; he nodded and took out a pen and a little waiter's notebook.

'What can I get you?'

Kat made herself laugh with the reply she thought up in her head, but she didn't say it, she couldn't, the reply she thought up was: some food garcon. Just so you I think garçon is French for boy. So, her reply to the waiter would've been some food, boy, I give up…He hadn't even done anything wrong, he was just doing his job…

But she didn't say that, oh no, they just ordered, you know, like normal customers, when they were done ordering, the waiter took their menus away. They didn't even order any drinks, but mind you, if drinks of the soft variety were all they were going to get, they weren't exactly bothered. When all the ordering was done, the waiter decided to leave them to it.

'OK, so I have two things I want to talk about tonight with you, preferably, in here…Amongst other people…'

'Yes, therapy was fine, wait two?'

'I miss you…'

Kat laughed, she actually found that funny. 'Miss me? Then why did you fuck up, not once but twice?'

'I don't know how to answer that, other than by saying I fucked up twice because I am a fuck up…But a fuck up who cares about you…'

She crossed her arms. 'No, you cannot say you're a fuck up and bring your depression into this…Not allowed, sorry…'

He put his hand outstretched on the table, in the hopes that she'd hold it, she didn't, obviously, 'Me saying that has nothing to do with my depression, I am a fuck up.'

'Well, I'm not going to argue with that…How can I?'

Dominic started laughing. 'But you love to argue!'

'Aw and you love to miss me!' Kat joined in with the laughter.

'I'm not even going to call that a joke because it's not, that was just inane babble and kind of cruel…'

'I apologise.'

'Apology accepted.'

They then moved onto talking about normal topics of conversation, like school, they both couldn't wrap their heads around Physics or maybe it was just the teacher, they both had the same awful teacher. They talked about the worst, they talked about the best, his favourite subject was History and hers was English, both essay subjects. Aw, even their favourite subjects have similarities! Then the very same waiter brought their food out, it looked good, good enough to eat! Wait, wasn't that the whole point?

The food was put on the table but before he had even started eating before he had even picked up his cutlery he said, 'I miss you.'

'Miss me? But I'm right here?'

'Miss being able to call you mine,' he lowered his voice. 'You have my virginity for Christ's sake, that shit means something to me…'

He then started eating his food, but she didn't.

'So where does that leave us?'

'Where do you want it to leave us?' he asked.

'No, don't give that bullshit about choice, I'm not in the mood.'

'OK, fair, let's go with hypothetically where are we?'

'The moon?' She laughed.

'Be serious, please.'

'OK, fine, where are we? A restaurant, oh look our foods here! Let's eat, I'm starving.' She picked up her fork.

'I know you really struggle with it, like really struggle, but please try and be serious, for me…For once in your life…'

'OK, fine. You want serious? I can be serious…OK, ready? Well, you're causing quite a large pain in my ass because I still love you.' She then started eating, but only because she needed to do something with her hands.

'How can you love a monster like me?'

'It's not like you've changed, you're still you, you're still the guy I feel comfortable enough to share my life story with, yes you made some mistakes, but I think you're beating yourself up about them far more than I ever could.'

'Feel? As in present tense?'

Kat stopped eating and held his hand that was still held out on the table, she looked into his eyes all seriously and said, 'No, future tense.'

He laughed. 'OK, I put my hands up to that,' and he did put his hands up, 'Good joke.'

'Um? But I make them all the time?' She laughed. 'Don't make such a big deal about one?'

'If you so choose to become a comedian, then just know that I'll be your biggest fan…'

'No, remember, I know you, you're only saying that because you want in my pants.'

'Wait, can you dot dot dot?'

'I bloody well believe so, it's my leg that's broken, not my vagina.'

Dominic laughed.

'Well done.' He kept on laughing, a tear even shed. 'The jokes are just flying out of you today, aren't they?'

They finished their food; their plates were taken away and the bill was brought. Dominic put his debit card on top of the bill to signify he was paying.

'I'm going to go to the loo, we didn't exactly order much, so contactless should work, do you mind tapping my card and paying?'

'Of course, I don't mind, go!'

But what she really meant was *of course I don't mind paying with my card, go! Off you trot to the loo…*

But Dominic left the table to go to the toilet, stupid boy, very soon after someone came to take a payment, so Kat got her card out and paid.

Dominic was on his way back up to the table when she paid, so he saw everything, he saw his debit card left on the table and started walking quicker. But the waiter was ready to leave when he arrived.

Upon seeing Dominic, the waiter said, 'Hey, cheers, look after her, yeah?'

'Oh, don't you worry, I plan to.'

'OK, have a lovely evening!'

Were the waiter's last words before he left.

Dominic sat down. 'I could've sworn you said, of course, I don't mind when I asked if you could pay with my card?'

'It's paid for, it's all sorted, done and dusted, calm down.'

'Calm down? I wanted to pay?'

'Pay next time? Or split it down the middle, I don't mind.'

'You're lucky I love you.'

'Love me? Are you sure?'

'Kat, that wheelchair turd, I, Dom one dick or Dom two dicks, love you excruciatingly deeply, with all the energy my weak, feeble heart can produce.'

Kat actually teared up at that.

She grabbed Dominic's hand and held it, in return, Dominic held hers back, she leaned her face closer to his.

'I think I love you too.'

That was when they kissed.

It actually felt electric, it sizzled. It was amazing, it was wonderful. It made them feel complete, they were two halves of a puzzle, in order to complete the puzzle, they needed each other, in order to feel complete within themselves, they needed each other. They just needed each other, there was no reason for it. Dominic put a hand on her face, Kat put a hand on his face. The kiss was strong and passionate, neither wanted it to end, but it was Dominic who pulled away first.

'My God, have I missed you. The waiting was killing me…'

Kat chuckled. 'No, no, no, you didn't miss me, you kissed me.'

'Seriously, where did that good joke come from earlier? I was actually impressed by it because that was, quite frankly, dreadful.'

Again Kat started laughing. 'The art of plagiarism.'

'Thought so…'

'Should we get a taxi to mine? I don't think I trust you wheeling me on public transport just yet, sorry.'

'We?'

'Remember, you have a phone, you can text my mum, it's not like I like spending time with you or anything...' Kat started laughing.

'Oh shit, of course...' Dominic also started laughing.

'Hey, can we please order a taxi to take us home?' Dominic asked a waitress who was just walking past.

'Yeah, sure, no worries, just write your destination here, we'll get that sorted out for you...' She pulled out a pen and her order book.

Dominic looked at the pen and paper and said, 'I'm not even going to pretend I know your address...'

Kat's laughter continued, 'Then give it here.' So, Dominic passed them over, Kat instantly wrote her address down, almost like it was her address and that's why it was so fast. Oh no wait, it was her address...

'Thank you,' Dominic said to the waitress.

'Yes, thank you, my crippled legs are nervous about using public transport.'

The waitress didn't know what to say to that, so she just walked away.

'Poor joke,' Dominic said.

'Joke? But it's honesty? Aw, do you find me so funny, that you think everything I say is a joke?'

'Just come here.'

So Kat leaned her face towards his.

This time it was Dominic who kissed Kat.

It was quite a long kiss, tongues were involved, it got messy, but why should they give a flying fuck? They needed each other, they had each other. They were both fucked up, royally fucked up, but not so much together...

'Um, sorry? Excuse me?' the same waitress who took their taxi order said, Kat and Dom, pulled their faces away from each other in not the most romantic or calm way.

'Um, yes?' Dominic said with a hint of anger in his voice because he was made to stop what he was doing…He was quite enjoying what he was doing…

'Taxi. Here.'

'OK, thank you,' Kat said in a sweeter way.

So, they put on their coats and left the restaurant, the waitress came outside with them because she knew which car was the taxi, she had been told the number plate.

'Appreciated,' Dominic said, he was finally more cheerful, well his voice was.

They quickly found the taxi, the waitress helped Dominic put Kat in the backseat, so the driver didn't have to move. Dominic put her wheelchair in the boot and sat next to Kat in the backseat, they were all ready to go. Kat first double-checked the driver had the right address, he did, so all was good in the world.

Chapter 22

They waved to the waitress as they drove off and that was it, they were gone.

'And how are we this evening?' the driver asked.

'Excited,' Dominic answered.

'Thrilled,' Kat said at the same time.

They both looked at each other and started kissing again. 'How sweet!' The driver said to himself, 'Young love.'

They didn't stop kissing for the whole drive there, then they arrived at her house. The driver got up to help Kat get back in her chair, Dominic had cash so he paid. She paid for food, he paid for taxi, that's equal, right? So the driver drove away.

'It would be so easy to sneak you in if I was able-bodied by the way.'

'But you're not, so another time?'

'There's a single disabled toilet cubicle like a one-minute walk away?'

'A toilet?'

'A cubicle.'

'Oh lord, are you feeling frisky by any chance?'

'After all that kissing, aren't you? Make-up sex is a thing, you know?'

She was sure she wouldn't be going inside her home anytime soon, so she rolled herself a cigarette, Dominic said nothing and just stared at her.

Fast forward to twenty minutes later.

Of course, they had reached the disabled toilet, could've put money on it, having sex in a wheelchair is difficult, but possible. By jove was it possible. Dominic moved in and out of her with force and she just kissed him. Then he finished, so he stopped and collapsed onto her, perks of having a wheelchair I guess.

'You know what? I don't think I just love you; I think I'm in love with you,' he whispered into her ear and kissed it.

She lifted his face up with her hand, so they were looking at each other. 'Then kiss me, on the lips,' she joined in with the whispering.

He did as he was told, he kissed her.

The kiss could've been for minutes…It could've been for hours…Time didn't matter anymore…They had each other and that's all they needed, it's all they wanted.

'You best not fuck up again, like even remotely,' Kat said after she moved her lips away from his and laughed.

'I'd rather die,' Dominic stated.

Kat laughed. 'Yes, I know you would, I don't have the memory of a goldfish, I remember meeting you.'

'You know what I mean…'

Kat kept the laughter going, 'Hmm, you know what, I don't know if I do…'

Dominic moved his fist up as if to punch her and just ended up stroking her face instead, he just wanted to touch her.

'You're lucky I love you…'

'Lucky is not the word I'd use to describe me, I'm sure there are better words…' She pointed to her wheelchair, 'I mean look at me!'

'I am looking at you, my God I am looking at you and the word beautiful doesn't even describe what I see.'

'I love you too,' Kat stated.

'You poor fucker. But how? Why? I'm the reason you're in this chair, it's my fault.' He teared up and started crying.

Kat just held him and put his ear close to her mouth, 'If it's your fault, the least you can do is help me out of it.'

'What now?'

'If you like, but my leg is still fucked so I'll need it back.'

That was it.

She had a task.

Get up.

Dominic stopped crying, stood up and got ready to hold her, he leaned forward and braced himself. 'OK, I'm ready when you are.'

Luckily, they were in a disabled toilet, so there were various poles attached to the walls Kat could hold onto for support.

'OK, I think I'm ready, don't hold me unless I need it, yeah?'

Dominic stopped leaning and jokingly said, ,'OK then, see you tomorrow,' and he started walking towards the door.

'Ha, funny!'

'Why thank you, I know I am.'

'No, but seriously stay.'

'I wouldn't miss this for the world.'

So, Kat got ready to stand up, there was a pole by the toilet, so she held onto it.

'Ready?' she asked Dominic.

'As I'll ever be,' was his answer.

So she did it, she stood up. Without Dominic's help.

Dominic started crying again, all he was able to say was 'wow.'

'I'm up!' Kat started crying too.

'Wow, yes, you're up…!'

'May as well do something useful while I'm up…'

'Oh God, like what?'

She just grabbed her catheter bag, opened it over the toilet and emptied out all her urine. Apparently, a girl can have sex with a catheter, so there…

'Ah, much better!'

'Doctor, help me out, I'm in love with a psycho.' Dominic laughed as he said it, good Kasabian reference, they're a band, if you don't know them, I give up…

'Psycho? But you love it really…'

'Yes, I do, I just said that.' He stopped laughing.

'Don't be mean.'

'I'm not being mean; I speak the truth.'

Her answer was just sitting back in her chair.

'Shall we go?' he asked.

'But I don't want you to have to go.'

'Will your parents let me in?'

'Don't see why not, it's not like I told them anything…'

'Why not? My fuck up seriously affected you?'

'We prefer to snort instead of talk.' Kat made herself laugh at that.

'OK, fair.' He tried but failed to say it seriously.

'I wouldn't say it's fair, but hey, that's life.'

They then left the toilet, went outside and went to Kat's house, Dominic rang the doorbell, there was no point in Kat having her keys, she didn't need them currently, it wasn't like she could open her door herself anyway…

It was the mother who opened the door. 'Jeez and what time do you call this? It's so late, I didn't realise therapy sessions were so long?'

'Sorry, I should've texted, we went to dinner,' Dominic said and casually missed out the having sex part.

'Aw, how lovely! Was it nice?'

'Well, it was fucking expensive and he made me pay!' Kat just about got the words out through laughter.

'Why you little…' He grabbed her head and pushed it down.

'Anyway, thank you, Dominic, for taking her…' the mother started.

'Actually, no, can Dominic come in? It's the least we can do.'

'Come in? But it's so late and you've got school tomorrow?'

'So late? Then let him sleep over?'

The mother thought for a moment.

'I think it's that wheelchair of yours that's softening me up, but fine, but Dominic let your mother know.' She stepped to the side to let them inside.

'Thank you so much,' Dominic said.

'Tom Hanks,' Kat said, you know basically thanks.

The mother laughed. 'You and your friends are like a big box of chocolates; you never know what you might get. A sweet comment or…I don't even know how to classify what you said Kat.' (If you don't understand that a big box of chocolates is a Forrest Gump joke because Tom Hanks played Forrest Gump, then I give up…)

They were now inside the house, so the mother closed the door.

'TV or game?' Kat asked Dominic, but it was the mother who replied straight away.

'You can do what you want obviously, but just know our dinner is in the oven and should be ready soon and we'll be watching TV,' is what she said.

'I think that means the right answer is game, so game?' was Dominic's answer, so Kat wheeled herself into the top Living Room, which only had a table and two sofas.

'I'll let you choose a game,' Kat said to Dominic while faced away from him because she was positioning herself in the Living Room, 'but only because they're downstairs.' She started laughing. 'Now, knowing you, you'll want to pick something shit, please don't.'

'How about I bring multiple options?'

'OK, yes, multiple options. Actually, no, stupid me for coming in here, open the door, let me out, I want a Blem.' Smoking was only allowed inside downstairs, so she had to go outside for one because they were upstairs.

'Can I leave you to it then? So I can check on food,' the mother said.

'Yes, of course, no worries and thank you again.' Aw, how sweet was Dominic? He truly was so grateful.

'No worries, but I warn you about playing games with this one, she must cheat…' She pointed to Kat.

Dominic just laughed and the mother went downstairs.

So, Kat wheeled herself to the front door, she took out her rolling materials, Dominic opened the door so Kat went outside and just started rolling.

Dominic started laughing, leaned in close to her ear and whispered the words, 'Cigarettes After Sex.'

'Good band,' was her answer.

'Wait you know them?'

Kat started laughing. 'No, sorry, who?'

'Can you please get a sense of humour?'

'I had one…Somewhere…I could've sworn I had one…'

She was then finished rolling, so she stuck the Blem in her mouth and lit it.

'I'll go on my quest for games in a sec, just let me send a text first.' So he, quite aggressively started typing.

Kat was too focused on her smoke to answer, so she said nothing. 'Is this OK?' he said.

'Is what OK?'

So, he read out the text that he'd just typed, 'May I stay at a friend's house tonight? We're doing a project for school and time got away from us.'

Kat started laughing. 'Hashtag friend zone.'

'No, but seriously, is it OK?'

'Well, if you were my kid, I'd allow you to spend the night elsewhere…What can I say? You're a trustworthy liar…'

'OK, cool,' he pressed send. 'All done! All sent! Are you good here? I'm going to go and find some games.'

'Am I good here? I can't exactly kill myself just outside my house, can I? Only slowly through cigarettes…So, not sure how good I am.'

'Poor, poor joke.'

'Joke? I'm not laughing?'

Dominic ignored that and just went inside the house to find some games, when he had found some he came back upstairs just as Kat was done with her smoke. He put the games down on the table in the upstairs Living Room and made sure Kat got in ok.

Upon reaching the upstairs Living Room, Kat closed her eyes, held her arms out and said, 'Whatcha got for me?'

The games Dominic brought were average, not shit, but not amazing, so Kat asked 'actually can we sit on a sofa and cuddle and talk?'

'Were the games I brought really that abysmal?'

'Here's a wild thought, ready?' Kat laughed. 'Maybe I just like you?'

'Wait. Wow. You like me?' Dominic joined in with the laughter. 'I knew you loved me, but my God? Like me? Is this a dream? Am I dreaming?'

'Just shut up and help me get on the sofa?'

So, he did as he was instructed and helped her onto the sofa and sat down next to her, she then moved so she was laid down on his lap, how sweet! She grabbed his hand and held it, he held hers back.

'Do today's events mean we're back together?' Dominic asked.

Kat sat up and looked at him, right into his eyes but still held onto his hand. 'I don't know, what do you want?'

It only took him about a second to answer. 'You,' was all he said.

'OK, but if you do anything even vaguely wrong again, just know, even our friendship is as good as gone.'

'No, if I do anything even vaguely wrong again, I'm as good as gone.'

'Easy way out, no, you'll deserve to suffer,' Kat stated.

'I love how I said I'll commit suicide and your argument is no, stay alive, it'll hurt more.'

'I speak ze truth!'

'Can't argue with that.' He kissed her lips, deeply and breathed all of her in.

'Hey, hey, boyfriend? Game?'

'Oof if I must,' he started laughing, 'and here are some I brought earlier.'

He moved Kat and stood up to again show Kat what he had brought. 'You choose, I'm not fussed,' was her answer.

So, he chose quick enough and helped Kat sit at the table, he sat opposite her, it was a fairly long game, but Kat won, obviously.

'As my prize for winning, can you go upstairs to my room and get me some pyjamas?'

'Of course, I can, where might I find them?'

'Cupboard by the door.'

'On it!' He kissed her forehead and left to go to her room.

Kat just waited patiently; it didn't take him very long to come back downstairs again. 'OK, I have two things to say…'

'So, say them…?'

'OK, one, it felt more than weird being back up there after last time…'

'Past tense, two, go.'

'How can you not care?'

'Because I live in the present tense, not the past. Now, are you going to tell me the second thing?'

'Yes, jeez, sorry miss.'

He pulled out some pyjamas that he was holding behind his back, they had Disney princesses on them.

'One pair for you and one pair for me.' Dominic smiled.

'Hashtag gay,' Kat said through laughter.

'Oh, shh, you're just jealous and I'm sorry? Gay? But I was inside you earlier?'

'Jealous? How? Jeez and charming…'

'Because I'm going to look so fetch.' (Oh my God, he was actually able to quote Mean Girls, that is not normal…)

'Impressive, why and how do you know Mean Girls?' But he ignored her. She laughed, 'How about you come over when you're sober?' (That's a joke because Come Over When You're Sober is the name of an album.)

He laughed, but did he understand the joke? Unknown.

'Do you want me or your mum to help you put them on?' he asked her.

'Not bothered. But the real question is do you feel able to do it?'

'Let me just go get your mum…' So, he went downstairs to get her, the father also came upstairs and him and Dominic got Kat down the stairs. Kat then went into the bathroom with her mother to get changed. Dominic was waiting right outside the bathroom and when the girls were ready to leave, they opened the door, they all swapped places with Dominic so he could also get changed and then Kat and her mother went into the downstairs Living Room. As soon as she got there, she asked her mum for a smoke, so her mum gave her one and Kat's dad decided to speak.

'Is Dominic staying the night?'

'I believe so, why?'

'Where is he sleeping?'

'Down here, with me.'

'No, he's not, upstairs.'

'Why?'

'To avoid any inappropriate behaviour…'

'Do you really think I can have sex in a wheelchair with a catheter?' Well, judging by earlier I'd say yes, yes you can.

'Good point, well made.'

It was then that Dominic entered the Living Room fully dressed in pyjamas and helped Kat to sit down on the sofa, it was so much more comfortable for her on the sofa than in the chair. Then Dominic sat down, so just like earlier on the sofa upstairs, Kat snuggled her head into his lap and held his hand. He stroked her face without thinking about it, it was borderline amazing how they just picked up where they left off…

The father wanted to make a comment about them, but didn't, he just put on a film. The film was average, nothing special, but they watched all of it. When it was over, the father decided it was time for bed, so the parents left and nothing more was said about the sleeping arrangements, thank God! So, Kat just laughed.

'What's the joke?' Dominic asked.

She carried on laughing. 'My dad,' still laughing… 'thinks, is worried that if we go to sleep together,' yet more laughter, 'we'll physically sleep together.' She just couldn't contain her laughter. 'And here's the best part, I said I physically can't even have sex because of my injuries,' last burst of laughter, I promise, 'and he believed me!'

'Not going to lie, you talking about sex is just making me want you…'

'Then take me…'

So he did, they both just loved being so close to each other, well he was inside her, so you can't really get any closer than that…He finished and just held her. No words were said, no words needed to be said. They laid like that for quite a while.

'I don't want to, but I need to go clean myself up,' Dominic at long last stated.

So Kat tried and succeeded to move herself. 'Hurry back.'

'Quite clearly I will,' Dominic said and stood up to go clean himself up in the bathroom, Kat just took a deep inhale of his aura.

When he was done, when he was all clean, he came back to the Living Room and sat down next to her on the sofa.

'Hey there! So that just happened, your father would not be happy…'

'Ha, no, he wouldn't, please pass me one of my mum's smokes?'

'Sure thing.' So, Dominic stood up and went to go get one, then he started laughing. 'Don't make me say it again,' he passed her a smoke.

'Yes, yes, Cigarettes After Sex, hilarious.'

'Yes, it is hilarious, I'm oh so glad you think so.'

For the next hour or so, they talked about everything and nothing, they were friends first and foremost, who just occasionally had sex. Kat fell asleep first, practically mid-conversation, so Dominic attempted to do the same. He firmly put his arms around Kat and held her. Then he tried and succeeded to fall asleep.

They were so sweet together, they needed each other.

Chapter 23

In the morning, the mother came down the stairs to wake them up.

'SCHOOL,' she shouted and clapped her hands 'SCHOOL,' and again 'SCHOOL,' and once more for good luck.

Dominic woke up first. 'Shh I'm trying to sleep, shh,' and he turned his head even further away from the mother and tried to fall back asleep.

The mother's answer to that was repeating what she had already said, but even louder, this time it worked, it woke both of them up.

'Oh God, it's Friday, Friday, gotta get down on Friday?' Kat said in a yawn (remember Rebecca Black's song Friday? Yeah, so does Kat…)

'Get down? No, get up!' The mother moved her arms up.

Kat and Dominic both grumbled, but they were awake now, so that was something…Kat buried her face into Dominic's shoulder.

'How did you two sleep?' the mother asked.

'Fine, but want, no need more,' was Kat's answer, well then it's your fault for staying up so late, isn't it?

'Shall we get you dressed in the Bathroom? Getting dressed and ready to start the day, may make you feel better.'

'Do I even have a choice?'

'Not really, no.'

Then without saying anything, Dominic heaved himself up and helped get Kat into her wheelchair, then they both got dressed for school, but in separate rooms, Kat in the Bathroom, Dominic in the Living Room. When they were both ready, they re-joined each other and had breakfast in the Kitchen.

Like usual, the father came down the stairs and sat at the Kitchen table, had a cigarette and had a mug of coffee when they were eating. 'Morning you two, how did you sleep?' he asked, see a perfectly nice question.

'Sleep? But we were busy banging all night? So didn't get any sleep...' Kat made herself laugh at that.

Dominic also laughed but tried to pass it off as coughing. Subtle.

So Kat, having now finished her breakfast, rolled herself a cheeky Blem and smoked it. When she was finished her father asked, 'School?'

'I'm sick of this whole going to school thing, how about we go to a theme park instead?' She laughed.

'Hmm because that would be illegal?'

Kat kept the laughter going at that. 'Like you give a shit about anything illegal? I mean come on...Seriously...?'

Dominic coughed again or did he laugh? Unknown.

The father ignored his daughter and again asked, 'School?' but he added a 'now.' So, why did he say it like a question? Unknown...This whole morning is filled with unknowns. I guess my characters are just mysterious mysteries...

So, Dominic stood up and Kat followed him towards the door, the father and Dominic helped her up the stairs.

But before they went upstairs, when they were still in the Kitchen, the father said to the mother, 'If Dominic's here we shouldn't need you to help with Kat, he can help, so you can stay here and start working...'

'OK, that's actually perfect, I have plenty of work to be getting on with here anyway so thank you, Dominic, I'll be getting on with that.' The mother then looked at Kat. 'See you later sweetie!' She waved.

So all the people who were leaving were now up and raring to go from the Kitchen table and ready to leave, so those who were able-bodied helped Kat up the stairs.

When they were up there, by the front door Dominic grabbed his school bag because Kat's was still at school in her form room where it was purposefully left yesterday and Kat and Dominic were ready to leave. The father grabbed his keys and he was also ready to leave. So they left the house and went to the car, Dominic helped the father get Kat in, then he got himself in, sat down next to Kat and held her hand softly. The father put her wheelchair in the boot and lowered himself down into the driver's seat of the car.

'Ready?' he asked.

'That depends, are we going to a theme park?' Kat asked but this time there was no laughter coming from her, it only came from Dominic, it was good to see he was feeling better, the coughing had subsided...

But the father just ignored her, pulled the car out of the driveway and said, 'Let's go!' So, off to school, they went...

The drive was average, they reached their destination, woo hoo! No crashes!

When they arrived, the dad and Dominic helped Kat get out of the car and into her wheelchair…Much to her dismay…

When she was all secure in her wheelchair, she said, 'Bye,' to her father, if only they both knew that was the last normal goodbye, he'd get out of her for a long old time…

The kids then went into school, like normal, hand in hand, wait was being hand in hand normal? At this point, I'd say yes, at this point in time they were happily together. They then separated, no they didn't split up…Geographically, they parted ways, not because they wanted to, but because they had to and then they went into registration, it was just a normal school day…Well, that was until it got to lunchtime…

Kat was on her way to get some food, all casually, when the Headmaster, yes, the Headmaster, tapped on her shoulder.

Nothing had even happened yet, but she knew this was strange, her and the Headmaster had never even had a basic conversation before. I mean what?

So, he asked, 'Not going to lie, I only knew it was you because of the wheelchair,' he laughed, who knows why he laughed, it's not exactly funny… 'But can we go and have a conversation somewhere more private?'

This spooked her, a conversation? But why?

'Do I even have a choice?'

That made him laugh. 'Just come with me,' he said and put his arms around her shoulders, for a second and led her to an empty classroom, but he didn't push her, which she was grateful for, he then just walked in front of her.

'You're successfully scaring me.'

'This is just quite serious, that's all, do you want a friend with you? I can get you a friend, if you like…'

'You asking me shit like that is moving me up from being scared to being terrified and yes, I just swore.'

'OK, shall I just start?'

'Yes, maybe.'

'OK.' He breathed in and breathed out as if trying to prepare himself, I'm sorry prepare yourself for what? It's her shit show of a life, not yours? 'Here I go…' Still stalling? Just get it out man? 'So I just got off the phone with Social Services…' Yes, carry on… 'Your parents have been arrested…' Yes, OK, complete the trilogy… 'I can't say the last part.' Come on, you're so close, 'And you've been taken into care…'

Kat was more than in shock at that, so she just left the classroom that she was in with the Headmaster, that was it, she needed a cigarette, so she plugged herself into her iPod and went to the front gate.

The Security Lodge said something like, 'Aren't you too young to leave?' As she left, but Kat didn't stop, why would she? Good to see the Security Lodge were doing their job, by stopping pupils that were too young to leave from leaving.

She had now walked far enough away from school, where no one could see her so it was only time for a safe Blem, so she rolled.

She rolled and smoked one Blem, then another, then another…

She knew whose fault this was, there was only one possible suspect and no it wasn't Dominic, so Kat angrily stormed herself back into school, well, she wheeled herself, to give her a piece of her mind…

There was only one person who knew Kat's address and who knew about the ins and outs of Kat's life, perks of being the ex-best-friend I guess, yes ex, Dominic may now be the boyfriend but before how could you not say he was the best friend? She told him everything for Christ's sake…But regardless of Dominic, if she did this, not only had she lost the best part from her title, she had also lost the friend part…

So, Kat stormed back into school, as angrily as she could in a wheelchair, she kept the rage up as she entered the Dining Hall, then she saw her.

Dominic was actually sat opposite from Juliet having lunch, how yin and yang, shame Kat didn't care about what they were talking about. Kat went over to them as quick as she could, but said nothing.

'Hello, sweetie,' Dominic said and kissed her on the cheek, Kat let him but didn't move, she just glared at Juliet. 'Do you want some lunch?' he asked.

'Not hungry,' she stated because how could she be? Kat started glaring and kept her glare fixed on Juliet.

'We were actually just talking about you,' Dominic said to Kat.

'I think she's spoken enough about me…' was Kat's answer.

'Shit, do you know? I was actually hoping to tell you this lunch or at least today…' Juliet finally spoke.

'Yes, I fucking know, the Headmaster took me to a fucking empty classroom at the start of lunch to tell me.'

'Shit.'

'Is an understatement.'

'I only did it because I care so much about you.'

'Great, well, next time just don't care and be apathetic because you've uprooted and fucked my whole life up.'

'Wait, what?' Aw, Dominic was so lost…

'You got them arrested, so I now live in an orphanage.'

'Wait, what?' Juliet was in clearly in shock, yeah, well, should've used your brain and thought, shouldn't you?

'What did you honestly think would happen by telling them?'

'Didn't think that far ahead…'

'No, you didn't think, did you?'

'Can someone please explain whatever is going on to me?' Dominic borderline shouted; he was worried it was going to get physical between them.

'I'll let Juliet explain it to you because she's oh so good at talking…Aren't you?' Kat leaned back in her chair.

Juliet tried to get herself ready to explain, but it didn't work. 'I can't,' she had started crying, 'I just can't.'

'No, don't give me that shit, just explain what you did, remember you're truly an expert at talking, so just explain…'

'OK,' she breathed, 'fine.'

'Should I be worried?' Dominic asked.

'No, don't worry, your family is fine…Just listen to what she has to say…' Kat stated to Dominic, her anger was still very apparent…

Juliet was now ready to speak, so she started speaking, 'So upon having a more than deep conversation with Kat the other day…' Juliet wiped her eyes.

'Yes, continue…' Kat stated.

'It just got me thinking, Kat needed help, I wanted to help her…'

'Getting Social Services involved is not helpful!'

'Wait, what?' This time it was Dominic who said it.

'Yes, this fucking idiot got Social Services involved in my life and as a result, my parents have been arrested and I now live in an orphanage, I'd rather live on the second star to the right and straight on until morning, but hey ho.' (A second star to the right and straight on until morning is a Peter Pan joke, you should really know that...)

'My fuck, are you even remotely, OK? No, but seriously, how can you make jokes in a situation like this?' Dominic stated.

'But I was being serious?'

'I love you.'

'Is that you also trying to create a joke?'

'Hey, don't be unnecessarily mean to me, I'm in your corner, I'm on your side, I'm more than mad at her, I'm just speechless...'

Kat started crying, 'Are you really on my side?'

'Yes, of course I am,' he held her hand, then looked at Juliet. 'What the actual fuck were you thinking?'

'I just wanted to help.'

'Surely you have enough brain cells to know that involving anyone, especially Social Services is not helpful?'

'Can we go sit somewhere else please? I don't want to look at her anymore,' Kat said, so Dominic stood up and left the table with Kat, they went to go sit at their usual table on the other side of the Dining Hall.

'I'm not even going to ask are you OK? That's a stupid question because I know you're not,' he held her hand, 'but can I help?'

Her tears were still flowing strongly. 'You can kill me.'

'No, see, Juliet I would kill—' he started laughing—'but not you.'

'What can I do to get you to kill me?'

His laughter continued. 'Become Juliet.'

Kat then made the conversation all serious again. 'I'm terrified, I've never even seen my new home, that's how new it is.'

'Shh, try not to worry, you're only sleeping there, so most of the time you won't even be awake in there.'

'Yeah, that is if I can even get to sleep in there…'

'Don't be silly, you will.' He moved his hand away from her hand, onto her face and gingerly stroked it.

'Don't call me silly,' she stated and wiped her eyes. 'Really not in the mood. Or is that silly? Am I being silly?'

'Of course not, my God, no wrong word on my part.' He lowered his face down and lowered the volume of his voice, 'Do you have a plan for after school?'

'I don't know, um, most likely I'll wait in reception for someone to pick me up and take me to my new home?'

'You shouldn't be on your own, I'll wait with you.'

'No, go home.'

'And leave you here, all alone? Facing the biggest life shake up since sliced bread? No thanks, I'd rather not.'

'Thank you, I think I'll need you.'

'Now, the bell is about to ring for the end of lunch, please eat something, but I'll see you at the end of school, yeah?'

'No to eating and yes but just so you know before going to reception and waiting, I'll need and want a cigarette, so I'll leave school then come back.'

'Thank you for telling me your after-school plan, can I accompany you on your smoky quest? Far more interesting than just waiting here.'

'I wouldn't have told you if I didn't want you to come?'

'I love you.'

'Very sweet, but I like you.'

Dominic laughed. 'Like me?' then the bell rang for end of lunch. 'Where shall I meet you at the end of school?'

'The moon?'

Dominic kept the laughter going. 'Don't start with that shit again.'

Kat also started laughing. 'Shit? But the moon is made of cheese?'

'Stahp.'

'OK, fine, by the entrance?'

'It's a deal, it's a steal, it's sale of the fucking century.' (He only went and bloody quoted the film Lock, Stock And Two Smoking Barrels, seriously if you've never seen it, watch it.)

'I love that you can quote *Lock Stock…*'

'Great film.'

'I'm aware…'

'Yeah well, I like you too.'

On that bombshell, the bell had rung approximately three hours before to signify the end of lunch, so they left the Dining Hall and went to registration. Maybe three hours is pushing it slightly, but I did say approximately so technically it's not a lie…Technically…Maybe, just maybe it was only a matter of minutes.

That afternoon's lessons went by really rather slowly for Kat, either way she only attended in body and not in mind.

She kind of had bigger things to think about and worry about at that moment in time…

Then she thought about the fact it was a Friday and what did her Fridays now usually consist of…? Cocaine and games…Hmm, no, not tonight, her normality had been arrested and fuck knows where she was even going because it wasn't home. She was homeless, she had no home…

Chapter 24

Then the final school bell rung, end of the day! Finally, home time! Or not…Kat had no home anymore…

But Kat wheeled herself to the exit of school, boy did she need a Blem now and waited for Dominic, it didn't take him long to show up, when he did, they threaded their hands together and left. Dominic now knew not to push her, so he didn't. As soon as they had left, like within seconds, Dominic was laughing.

'What's so funny? Do I even want to know?' Kat asked, she almost stopped moving forward, but didn't, making some dumb point was not as important as having a smoke.

Dominic just kept on laughing, until eventually he said, 'I've only gone and bloody confirmed it,' then his laughter took over again.

'Confirmed what? Words? Use them?'

They then reached somewhere far enough away from school where Kat could smoke, so she got out her rolling utensils and started rolling.

When she was rolling, was when Dominic decided to speak, 'So, people in my year now know I'm going out with an older lady.'

'Older lady? What? Why? It's not like I'm a cougar?'

'Older school year makes you older, so I described you as an older lady, but damn should've used the word cougar…Next time, I guess…' His heavy laughter appeared again, so Kat purposefully dropped her freshly rolled cigarette.

'Ugh, please help me, can you please pick up my smoke for me? I think it's by my feet, I dropped it…'

'Aw, does little old lady struggle to bend over?'

'Well, given I'm in a wheelchair, yes, yes I do.'

'Yes, of course, no worries,' he said as he bent over to look for the Blem.

Kat lifted up her good leg, but not to help him search, oh no, but he probably thought that was the reason.

'Found it yet?' Kat asked because if she didn't ask, she'd laugh.

'When I find it, you'll be the first to know, yeah?'

Kat originally wanted to wait until he'd found it, but upon hearing that she was worried that would be leaving it too late. So she moved her good foot up further so it was over his head and pushed down with all her might.

'Ouch, stop?'

'OLDER LADY? COUGAR?' Kat shouted.

'But you are older?' He started laughing again. 'In fact, too old to be smoking, think of your poor old lungs.'

'What?'

But he had gotten himself back up, grabbed Kat's wheelchair and started wheeling them back into school. The Blem may have been gone, but not forgotten…

Kat folded her arms and practically screamed rather grumpily, 'Why?'

'You may not care about your lungs, but I do.'

'At least let me wheel myself?'

'Oh, what and let you wheel yourself back and have a smoke? Nice try, but I don't trust you…This is for your benefit?'

Kat didn't even respond; she just didn't fight him in wheeling her back into school and into reception.

When they arrived there, there was already a lady sat in there, in a few minutes she decided to ask, 'Um, Kat?'

But Kat just ignored her because if this lady wanted her, she probably worked with Social Services, so Kat didn't want to speak to her, she just wanted a smoke…

But Dominic didn't ignore her. 'Yes, this here is Kat and I'm Dominic, are you taking her to her new home by any chance?'

Kat glared at Dominic; oh boy, did she glare. What was she hoping for anyway? For him to just stay silent?

'Thank God, the wheelchair was a bit of a giveaway…So, Kat, are you ready to go to your new home?'

'Home? Really?' She laughed. 'I've never even been there though. Doesn't sound like a home to me…'

'She's just nervous, understandably so,' Dominic started. 'Can I come with you and see she settles herself in, OK?'

'You really don't have to do that, this is my shit show of a life, not yours,' Kat said to Dominic, they were the only two people in the room, as far as Kat was concerned.

Dominic's gaze focused on Kat. 'No, it's our life, we're just experiencing some changes right now…' Then, his gaze moved to the lady, 'So, can I?'

'It's not conventional, but yes, I suppose so.'

'Perfect, ready when you are,' Dominic said.

'But I'm not…' Kat said, but she was ignored.

'OK, cool, my car is parked on the road outside.'

'But I'm scared of cars?' Again Kat was ignored, then they started the short walk towards her car, if Kat was just going to be ignored, she wanted to see how far she could take this. 'Dominic, I think I'm gay.'

'Aw, how sweet,' he answered.

'Sweet? Wait, what do you think I said?'

'That you want to lay in bed?'

'I have no words.'

They then arrived at the lady's car and lifted Kat into it.

'Actually, thank God you're here, I don't know how we would've got Kat into the car otherwise, didn't think,' the lady said to Dominic and joined Kat in the car, so that meant it was up to Dominic to put the wheelchair into the boot of the car.

So, he wheeled it and went to try and put it in the boot. 'You kind of need to unlock it,' he shouted to the lady.

'Oh God, I'm so sorry, not used to wheelchairs…'

'Well, get used to them,' Kat said and the lady got up from the car, ignored Kat and went to go assist Dominic with the boot.

When they were all sitting in the car, the lady said 'OK, formal introductions time! My name is Lily. Kat, I'm your key worker, if you have any problems, text me.' She took her phone out.

'Text you? On what?'

'Do you not have a phone?'

'It, like me, died in my fall.'

'Shall we get you a new one?'

'Nah, let me live my life off the grid.'

'Then how will we find you at the end of the school day?'

'We found you easily today, without phones, so reception?'

'I'd rather you had a phone, but this must be an awful lot for you to handle so I'm going to give you a reluctant OK, but we'll have weekly meetings, yeah?'

'Weekly meetings? What are you? A therapist?'

'Weekly meetings are quite regular?'

'Don't worry, I know, I'm just messing with you.'

'Ay, be nice, this is a shit situation for all involved,' Dominic whispered into Kat's ear, so only she could hear.

'Sorry, that was unnecessary for me to say,' was Kat's apology, Dominic's words had actually made her apologise!

'Please don't worry, I know this must be a lot,' Lily said.

Kat actually started laughing at that. 'That's an understatement and a half.'

Instead of saying anything Dominic just hit her square in the shoulder.

'Um? Ow?'

'Sorry, you had a mosquito on you.' Good lie but unbelievable...

So Kat decided to be quiet...

Lily, then, started driving, to Kat's new home...

The drive wasn't very long at all, less than ten minutes had passed and they were there, they had arrived.

Kat was put into her wheelchair, so now they were all ready and outside.

'Please, Doctor Dominic, can I have a smoke before going inside?'

Dominic just laughed. 'You are your own woman, you can do what you want?'

'You fucker, don't act all nice just because she's here,' Kat pointed to Lily.

Kat pointing at Lily woke her up from her daydream, so she spoke, 'Yes, of course, you can have a cigarette, this is your home after all.'

'OK, cool,' she started rolling, 'and what about smoking or taking anything else of the illegal persuasion…?'

'Shit I didn't even think maybe I shouldn't have said yes to smoking, I forgot you were underage, but strictly prohibited, obviously.'

'Then this place couldn't be more different from my real home if it tried.' She was done rolling, so she stuck the Blem in her mouth and lit it.

'Just try and be positive, if you have a good mindset then all this change will feel better hopefully,' Dominic said and gave Lily the biggest hug, OK, fine, not Lily, he hugged Kat, but did I catch you out?

'Change? BUT I DON'T WANT CHANGE?' Kat shouted.

'Can I interrupt?' Lily asked.

'Why bother asking? You're going to speak anyway? And anyways, I'm done speaking…' Kat said with a degree of anger.

'Um, OK, yes, so I've booked you in to see your parents tomorrow, they're obviously in different facilities but it should be nice to see them, well I'm hoping it will be…I'm guessing you're looking forward to it…?'

'Next time, tell me before you book anything, yeah? I'm the reason they're there, so no, I wouldn't say I'm excited,' Kat said, all emotion had left her voice, had left her body, it hurt too much. 'So, I'm understandably quite a bit scared…'

'Oh God, I didn't even think, sorry.'

'There seems to be a theme occurring here with you and not thinking…'

Kat was finished with her smoke, so she stubbed it, Lily just ignored what Kat had said, so she just instead asked, 'Shall we go in?'

'Do I even have a choice?'

'Not really, no.'

'Then yes I would love to,' Kat said with as much seriousness as a chocolate teapot and walked to the entrance.

Lily rang the doorbell; it took a few minutes for a middle-aged woman to open it. 'Two? I could've sworn you only said one on the phone…'

'Yes! Don't worry! Only one! This is just her friend, he's lovely, I'm guessing you'll be seeing quite a lot of him…'

'Hopefully,' Dominic said, but at that moment Kat had quickly wheeled herself towards the front gate, she was out of there.

Dominic sprinted after her. 'PLEASE COME BACK, DO THIS, I BELIEVE IN YOU, YOU'RE THE STRONGEST PERSON I KNOW,' he shouted after her.

She stopped moving, she stopped trying to escape, well she just stopped.

She turned around and said, 'You what?'

He approached her slowly when he reached her, he put a hand on her face and said, 'You are,' he started stroking her face, 'the strongest person I know.'

'The strongest? But I'm so weak?' She started crying.

'Weak? Don't lie to me.'

'I'm gross, what did I do to deserve you?'

'Gross?' He started laughing. 'My God, yes, you may be strong, but boy do you need a wash…I can smell you from here…'

'Well, you are directly in front of me, don't hate or rather don't smell the player if you can't smell the game.'

'You're lucky I like you, like I can tolerate you…'

Kat laughed. 'Wow, I didn't realise I was going out with the definition of romance.' She kissed him, he kissed her, the feelings were mutual.

He stopped the kissing first, Kat was a bit miffed, she could've gone on for longer, well forever preferably, she didn't want to go back to the orphanage.

'I know you don't want to, but can we go back? I'm not leaving until you have a roof over your head.'

'Poor, poor choice of words, then don't leave, I don't mind.'

'Let's face this, it's just another obstacle in the saga known as your life.'

'Saga?'

'Yeah, I think we're on the fifth book now,' Dominic started laughing. 'I think we've beaten *Lord of the Rings;* it only took Frodo three books to destroy *The Ring of Power.*'

'You're more than strange.'

He bent over backwards, so he looked more than strange coincidentally. 'I'm not strange, I'm yours.'

'Oh yeah, don't remind me…'

But they walked back to the orphanage, well Dominic walked and pushed the wheelchair, coincidentally, he didn't trust Kat not to wheel herself away again, probably just as well because Kat didn't trust herself either…

When they arrived again at the orphanage, Lily and the woman were in some deep conversation, it was like they'd never even left, they both huffed as they spoke.

Until Lily said, 'OK, Dominic, let's go now.'

'Go? Can't I at least see her inside?'

'Not if you want a lift with me, you can't.'

'But I don't even know where I am?' Was his argument, it was so poor I don't even know if you could call it an argument.

'No, you go, my sweetie, I've got her now,' the orphanage lady said to Dominic.

Lily started walking back to her car and Dominic followed.

She shouted back to Kat. 'See you tomorrow,' and waved.

Whereas Dominic just cleared his eyes of tears, it was so sweet how much he cared about Kat, then they were both in the car, so Lily started driving.

'We knew you were in a wheelchair, so we shuffled some stuff around and you've got a bed downstairs.' She moved herself and ushered Kat inside.

So Kat went inside. 'Um, so what's your name?' Kat asked the lady.

'Oh oops, have I not introduced myself? It's Hannah.'

'I assume you know who I am, but how many other kids live here?'

'Well, you make it a lucky half dozen.'

'OK, so ages?'

'You would be the oldest by five years or so…'

'Fucking fantastic.'

'Please don't worry you can always talk to me.'

'Oh, really? You'd do that? You'd talk to me?'

'Now, there's no need to be rude, we're your family now.'

'Oh, joy.'

Then they got to what Kat assumed was her room, well it was downstairs with a bed.

'Can you please help me get in bed?'

'Bed? But it's so early? What about dinner?'

'My whole life has more than drastically changed, somehow I don't feel like missing one meal will kill me.'

'Don't you want to meet your new brothers and sisters though?'

'Are they going to die tonight?'

'W…w…what?'

Kat raised her voice, 'ARE THEY GOING TO DIE TONIGHT?'

'N…n…no.'

'OK, then I can meet them tomorrow.'

'Y…y…yes.'

'S…s…stop st…st…stuttering.'

So Hannah stopped talking and helped get Kat in bed.

'T—t…thank you,' Kat said and turned away from Hannah.

'Happy now?' Hannah asked.

'Jeez, you only helped put me in bed, you haven't even started on my problems, but will you ever? Unknown.'

'Shall I just go?'

'Bye…' Kat even waved.

Hannah just shut Kat's door, collapsed onto the floor and started crying. It was obvious Hannah didn't know how to deal with teenagers, let alone ones who were quite as messed up as Kat, Hannah put her head in her hands. Meanwhile, on the other side of the door, in bed, Kat was also crying, she wished Dominic was there, he had a knack for making her feel better.

It took her ages to fall asleep and by ages, I mean ages, like hours, one it was early when she got in bed and two she was just thinking and overthinking. But eventually, she fell asleep, oh how she wished it was for forever…

Chapter 25

When Kat awoke the next day, oh boy did she groan, there was a clock by her bed which read a humble quarter to six in the morning, oh joy! Not only was it ridiculously early but she was stuck in bed until someone could get her up, she made a mental note to herself, she needed a TV or something to do in this room that was now hers...

So, she did all she could do, she just lay there, she didn't even have a book to read, she tried and failed to fall back asleep. Lord only knows how long she just lay there for, but I think we were approaching the three-hour mark...

Then Hannah came into and entered the room, 'Oh, good you're awake, Lily's on her way for your outing today!'

'I have two things to say to you...'

'Is one of them good morning?'

'Not quite, no.'

'Ugh, why am I not surprised? But OK, fine, lay it on me,' Hannah said and went to go open Kat's curtains.

'OK, ready? Well, one, I need a TV or something I can do in here, I've literally just been laid here awake for hours, with just my thoughts to keep me company, which aren't exactly happy at the moment...'

'Not sure how I feel about you having a TV in your bedroom…'

'Seriously? Why not? It's not going to kill me, I think I've already proven I'm quite resilient, I mean look at me.' Kat pointed at herself and at her wheelchair. 'I can't even kill myself…Oh, how I've tried…'

But Hannah just ignored that. 'OK and number two?'

'OK, fine, ignore me, I don't mind. But two, you can't exactly call where I'm going an outing? It's not like we're going to the park?'

There was a chair in the room, so Hannah went to go sit in it, she lay back in it and said, 'I can't help but feel you hate me, why? Why do you hate me? What have I done wrong? I've only tried to be nice…?'

'I don't hate you; you seem lovely, I just hate life.'

'My God, my little cherub, I know you've been through it,' she held Kat's hand, 'but just know, I'm here for you.'

'Don't. Stop. You'll make me cry.'

Hannah laughed. 'I think we've found you a nickname, cherub?'

Kat also laughed. 'Ha no, I wish I were a cherub, to be a child secret agent would be so cool.' (That's a joke about the Cherub books by Robert Muchamore, if you haven't already put this down and read them.)

But Hannah didn't understand the joke either, 'Huh?'

'Never you mind, but can you please help me get in my chair? I'm starving, I need to get up, I need breakfast.'

'Yes, of course, that's why I came in here.'

'Appreciated.'

So, Kat lifted herself up a little bit and Hannah picked her up. 'Ready to meet your new family? They're having breakfast too.'

Kat was now in her wheelchair and started wheeling herself out of her room. 'Well, even if I say no, I'm meeting them anyway…'

'Just try and be nice, my little cherub.'

'You know what? No, call me Kat, if I can't keep my parents, I can at least keep the name they gave me.'

'Your choice, obviously.'

Then they arrived at a closed door, Hannah put her hand on it and got ready to open it. 'Are you ready?'

Kat just stared at her.

'No, stupid question, of course you're not ready, but food, sustenance well breakfast is through here.'

Hannah just opened the door.

Kat wheeled herself inside.

'Hey guys, good morning! So this girl right here is your new older sister,' Hannah said and pointed to Kat.

There was another adult in there overseeing breakfast. 'Hi, I'm Stephanie, nice to meet you, not going to lie I'm grateful you're older, finally someone I can have a conversation with.'

Kat took that as the perfect time to make a joke, she just pointed to herself and put a finger over her mouth to signify she couldn't speak.

'Oh shit, I'm so sorry, can't you speak?'

Kat just shook her head.

'Oh, come off it, you can speak just fine,' Hannah said.

'She's right, walking no, talking yes.'

Stephanie laughed. 'Good joke.'

So, Kat positioned her wheelchair at the table and poured herself a bowl of cereal and started eating it, not much more was said until a child decided to speak, she was quite young, maybe about five or so.

'Why is she always sat down?' she asked Stephanie.

'Sorry,' Stephanie mouthed to Kat.

But Kat didn't mind at all, so she answered, 'I fell! Whoops! I think I'm more than clumsy! Aren't I silly?'

'Will you ever be normal?'

'Hopefully...'

That was when the doorbell rang, it certainly saved Kat from that conversation, not that she needed saving, it was only with a child...But it wasn't exactly the most comfortable of conversations...

'Let me go get that, it'll probably be Lily,' Hannah said and went to the front door, she answered it, said a few words and came back into the Dining Room, with you guessed it, Lily.

'How are you this morning?' Lily asked Kat.

Kat put another mouthful of cereal in her mouth. 'Hungry,' she just about got the word out coherently, well Lily understood it.

'How are you feeling about today?'

Kat started laughing. 'Like a weight-watcher in a sweet shop.'

'I'm sorry, what?'

'All over the shop.'

'That's understandable.'

'Oh, is it? So why are we going?'

'At the end of the day, they are your parents and you're their child...'

'Ugh, OK, so let us go then, get this over with.'

So, Lily got up, walked to the front door of the house and then to her car. Kat and Hannah followed her.

'Give me a hand getting Kat into the car please,' Lily asked Hannah, it was nice to see them being civil with each other today. They quickly loaded Kat into the car, put the wheelchair into the boot and Lily got into the car.

'Ready?' Lily asked and the car started moving.

'I'm not even going to satisfy that with a response.'

'So, yes?'

'If you want...' Kat said and stared out the window.

'Dad first.'

'Joy.'

They drove along for who knows how long, but in silence and then they arrived. 'I'm just going to go get someone to help me get you into your chair.'

'OK, thanks for asking me how the orphanage is.'

But Lily just ignored that, got out of the car and left, in only a matter of minutes she returned with someone to help get Kat in her chair. When she was in her wheelchair, she stated 'smoke first, visit after.'

'Thanks for all your help, we're all good now,' Lily said to the helper.

So, like usual, Kat rolled and smoked.

'Just know this is huge, how are you feeling?'

'Peachy.'

'Are you lying by any chance?'

'Rude, how dare you call me a liar, I'm a truther.'

'And I was going to ask you how the orphanage was.'

'Ha, is that so?'

'Yes.'

'Maybe next time tell someone that believes you.' Kat stubbed her Blem. 'So, I guess we should go in?'

'Yes, let's.'

So, Lily walked to the entrance and Kat rolled.

When they entered, Lily went over to the reception, spoke quietly and re-joined Kat.

'Someone should be coming to help us soon.'

In a matter of minutes, a uniformed officer came over to talk to them, well he whispered something in Lily's ear.

'Won't come out? What do you mean won't come out? This is a prison and you're an officer, can't you do something? This is his daughter for Christ's sake!'

'Sorry, madam, but no.'

'Um, hello? Talk to me? Involve me! It's my life!'

'Sorry, you're involved, trust me you are…' Lily said.

'Does my dad refuse to see me?'

'I'm so incredibly sorry, but yes.'

Kat tried to stop them, but tears fell down her face.

'Don't mind me, I'm just going out for a smoke.' But she lied, it wasn't just a smoke, she had four in quick succession, Lily carried on having an angry conversation with the guard but upon repeatedly being told that he couldn't help her, she stormed outside.

'What a fucking joke!' Lily breathed the words out.

'Just think, if they forced him to see me, it wouldn't have exactly been a happy meeting, it's better off this way.'

'How are you so calm?'

'So much shit has happened in my life, I just don't care anymore.'

'You're far too young to be saying that…'

'But it's true, age doesn't come into it.'

That was it, Lily started crying.

In between a sob Lily said, 'Let me just go get someone to help get you in the car.'

So Lily left, she went into the reception, sat down, had a five-minute breather and then eventually asked for someone to help her with Kat. When they were all loaded into the car with all their belongings, they waved bye to the helper and left.

'Where to now?'

'I don't think I can take anymore parent drama today, so orphanage? I refuse to call it home,' Kat stated.

'You poor thing or Dominic's? I know where he lives now.'

'Fuck, yes please, Dominic's.'

'On it.'

Chapter 26

So, Lily sped along on the road, she knew her destination.

'How long until we get to our destination?'

Lily, stupidly turned around and faced Kat to answer, 'About...'

That's as much of her answer that came out because another car rammed into her and she crashed. Oops.

Silence ensued for the longest time, well forever for Lily because she passed away, she was hit too hard, the car spun, oh boy, did it spin. Another car had hit it in the side, it pushed and pulled Kat in all sorts of directions, all she could do was go with it, the force was too strong for her to fight. If this could be the end, Kat was happy about it.

Then she lost consciousness.

Who knows how long it had been, but she woke up with some paramedics from an ambulance trying to resuscitate her. She was on an ambulance bed with two pads stuck to her body, sending a current through her, a defibrillator.

'Hey...Hey...Stop...She's coming to...'

'Wha...what happened?'

'You were in a car crash, your friend, the lady driving, didn't make it...'

'Lily? What?'

'Let's get you into the ambulance.'

'Shit, my boyfriend?'

'What's his number?'

'I...I...I don't know, I don't have it...'

'What about the lady who was driving?'

'Possibly, but how am I supposed to know her phone passcode.'

One of the paramedics sprinted out of Kat's eye line and returned quite quickly.

'Brick Nokia, thank God, so no passcode needed.'

Kat laughed. 'My God, am I lucky or am I lucky?' The paramedic who had the phone passed it to her.

'Well, given you were just in quite a serious car crash, I'm going to vote for neither of the above...' he said.

The paramedics then put Kat in the back of the ambulance, when she was all secure, the one who was driving got in the driver's seat and the other sat in the back with Kat.

'Where are we even going? She has my boyfriend's number, so I can text him and tell him where we're going.' She had gotten the phone ready to text him.

'I can send the address as a text for you if you like?' the paramedic who wasn't driving said and held out his hand to hold the phone.

'Go for it,' Kat passed him the phone.

He instantly started aggressively typing where they were going, then he passed the phone back to Kat. He was done. 'I just sent the address of the hospital we're going to and the words come now all capitalised.'

Kat started laughing. 'That's only going to freak him the fuck out.'

'To be fair, you're not in the clear yet; yes, you're awake which is good, but I'll be much happier when you get through the next twenty-four hours...'

Kat then received a text from Dominic, it said *on my way.*

She could relax now, so she did, she shut her eyes and may have fallen asleep or passed out, whatever you want to call it...

When she awoke, the sun was rising, it was very, very early morning of the next day, Dominic was there, asleep, sat in a chair with their hands threaded together. He was practically in bed with her, he was leant over that much. How sweet!

There was only one way she thought was appropriate to wake him up, no, not through copious amounts of kisses, through a wet willy.

So, she gave him one.

'NO, BUT I LIKE YOU,' he shouted, then he came to, blinked, properly woke up and grabbed his now wet ear.

'Oh, my good God, were you dreaming about me?' Kat said and pulled her finger out his ear and moved her hand to cradle his face.

'Why? My ear?' He was slowly but surely waking up.

She laughed. 'I was just washing it?'

'Well, don't next time, yeah?'

'But it was so dirty?'

'Leave. It.'

'OK, OK,' she put her hands up.

'Anyway...You really scared me yesterday, I tried to wake you up when I arrived here, but you were just passed out.'

'Sorry.'

'No, shut up, don't be sorry, it was just an awful accident, a truly, terrible awful, awful accident, we lost Lily.'

Well, that only went and started Kat crying, 'I know.'

'How do you feel?'

'Well, I have felt better, it must be said.'

'Well, hopefully, the medication the doctor has given you will go into your arteries and get sucked up by your heart to get rid of your pain.'

Kat laughed. 'No, it's veins that suck stuff into your heart, arteries carry it away, it even says it, vein says in, artery starts with a so away, hashtag GCSE101.'

'How can you make jokes, right now, in a hospital bed, seriously?'

'Jokes? Can you not handle the truth or something?'

'My God, do I like you.'

At that, Kat grabbed and held onto Dominic's hand.

'Wait, what have you done wrong now? There's a strong positive correlation between my hospital visits and your fuck ups…'

Dominic laughed. 'No, this time you made it all the way to hospital by yourself, without my help, congratulations!'

'I see you've acquired a sense of humour, well done.'

'I try.' Once again they kissed.

'Ow, my head really hurts, I think I need more painkillers…' Kat said when the kiss concluded and held onto her head.

'On it, my like.' He kissed her quickly; you know just a peck and went to go get a Nurse.

'You're my absolute,' Kat said before he left 'my everything.'

'Good, glad to hear it's not one-sided.' He kissed her.

She sat back and tried to get comfortable, when all of a sudden, she started shaking, well seizing but this time not because of antidepressants and she passed out.

When Dominic came back into Kat's room, it was with a Nurse, thank God, Dominic panicked and ran over to Kat.

'WHAT DO I DO?' he screamed.

'L...L...Let me go, get some help,' the Nurse said and left.

Only minutes passed, but it felt like hours. Kat then stopped shaking and according to the beeps coming from the machine, she stopped breathing too.

The Nurse then came back in with a doctor.

But it was too late.

She was gone.

All Dominic could do was hold the corpse.

She passed away because of a brain haemorrhage.

Chapter 27

In a few days, it was the funeral.

Dominic didn't want to go, but he knew he had to. He knew he should. It was the least he could do for her.

When he was there, he got up and went to the front of the crowd because it was now his turn to speak. To a room full of silence, it must be said he wished there was chatter, something, anything to drown out the sound of his heart beating.

'I love her.' He started crying, 'No, I loved her.'

What could he even say to a Church full of people? Some he knew, from school, but most he didn't, family he guessed.

'I hope she's happier, wherever she is…'

I think it was obvious he hadn't prepared for this, but it didn't matter.

He turned around to the coffin. He put a piece of paper on it, a poem he'd written, how sweet! It said…

We're disgustingly similar, you're just like me, but now you're gone, forever I want to lay in bed. If I was suicidal before, then now I'm just dead, my heart is so heavy it feels just like lead.

Death would actually be positive because then I'd be with you. But no not really, yes it would get rid of my pain, but there's nothing anyone can do.

You've been through enough pain, just rest my beautiful girl. Give sleeping forever a good whirl.

'I like you.' He whispered those three magic words.

'I'm sorry, but why is her funeral being held in a fucking Church? She was atheist or now that she's gone, does it not matter what she would've wanted?' He said louder and started to walk outside. 'I just can't, I'm sorry.'

When he was outside, he took in a deep breath.

Then to nothing, he shouted, 'YOU BASTARD, FOR GETTING WHAT YOU WANTED, WHAT ABOUT ME AND WHAT I WANT? I WANT YOU.' He collapsed.

Then after a few minutes he decided to go for a walk, just around.

For Dominic, life was now about the journey, rather than the destination. Even breathing was a journey…

The End

Milton Keynes UK
Ingram Content Group UK Ltd.
UKHW050336201123
432823UK00021B/256

9 781528 969413